Life, The Universe
and Everything

Books by Douglas Adams

The Hitchhiker's Guide to the Galaxy
The Restaurant at the End of the Universe
Life, the Universe and Everything
So Long, and Thanks for All the Fish
Dirk Gently's Holistic Detective Agency
The Long Dark Tea-Time of the Soul
Mostly Harmless
The Salmon of Doubt
The Ultimate Hitchhiker's Guide to the Galaxy
The Original Hitchhiker Radio Scripts
The Meaning of Liff *(with John Lloyd)*
Last Chance to See *(with Mark Cowardine)*
The Deeper Meaning of Liff *(with John Lloyd)*

DOUGLAS ADAMS

Life, The Universe and Everything

 BALLANTINE BOOKS • NEW YORK

2005 Del Rey® Books Trade Paperback Edition

Published in the United States by Del Rey® Books, an imprint
of The Random House Publishing Group, a division of
Random House, Inc., New York.

Del Rey is a registered trademark and the Del Rey colophon is a
trademark of Random House, Inc.

Originally published in the United States by Harmony Books,
a division of Crown Publishers, Inc, 1982.

ISBN 0-345-41890-5

Printed in the United States of America

www.delreybooks.com

9 8 7 6 5 4 3 2 1

For Sally

Chapter 1

The regular early morning yell of horror was the sound of Arthur Dent waking up and suddenly remembering where he was.

It wasn't just that the cave was cold, it wasn't just that it was damp and smelly. It was that the cave was in the middle of Islington and there wasn't a bus due for two million years.

Time is the worst place, so to speak, to get lost in, as Arthur Dent could testify, having been lost in both time and space a good deal. At least being lost in space kept you busy.

He was stranded on prehistoric Earth as the result of a complex sequence of events that had involved his being alternately blown up and insulted in more bizarre regions of the Galaxy than he had ever dreamed existed, and though life had now turned very, very, very quiet, he was still feeling jumpy.

He hadn't been blown up now for five years.

He had hardly seen anyone since he and Ford Prefect had parted company four years previously, and he hadn't been insulted in all that time either.

Except just once.

It had happened on a spring evening about two years ago.

He was returning to his cave just a little after dusk when he became aware of lights flashing eerily through the clouds. He turned and stared, with hope suddenly clambering through his heart. Rescue. Escape. The castaway's impossible dream—a ship.

And as he watched, as he stared in wonder and excitement, a long silver ship descended through the warm evening air, quietly, without fuss, its long legs unlocking in a smooth ballet of technology.

It alighted gently on the ground, and what little hum it had generated died away, as if lulled by the evening calm.

A ramp extended itself.

Light streamed out.

A tall figure appeared silhouetted in the hatchway. It walked down the ramp and stood in front of Arthur.

"You're a jerk, Dent," it said simply.

It was alien, very alien. It had a peculiar alien tallness, a peculiar alien flattened head, peculiar slitty little alien eyes, extravagantly draped golden robes with a peculiarly alien collar design, and pale gray green alien skin that had that lustrous sheen about it that most gray green races can acquire only with plenty of exercise and very expensive soap.

Arthur boggled at it.

It gazed levelly at him.

Arthur's first sensations of hope and trepidation had instantly been overwhelmed by astonishment, and all sorts of thoughts were battling for the use of his vocal cords at this moment.

"Whh . . . ?" he said.

"Bu . . . hu . . . uh . . ." he added.

"Ru . . . ra . . . wah . . . who?" he managed finally to say and lapsed into a frantic kind of silence. He was feeling the effects of not having said anything to anybody for as long as he could remember.

The alien creature frowned briefly and consulted what appeared to be some species of clipboard that it was holding in its thin and spindly alien hand.

"Arthur Dent?" it said.

Arthur nodded helplessly.

"Arthur *Philip* Dent?" pursued the alien in a kind of efficient yap.

"Er . . . er . . . yes . . . er . . . er," confirmed Arthur.

"You're a jerk," repeated the alien, "a complete kneebiter."

"Er . . ."

The creature nodded to itself, made a peculiar alien check on its clipboard and turned briskly back toward its ship.

"Er . . ." said Arthur desperately, "er . . ."

"Don't give me that," snapped the alien. It marched up the ramp, through the hatchway and disappeared into its ship. The ship sealed itself. It started to make a low throbbing hum.

"Er, hey!" shouted Arthur, and started to run helplessly toward it.

"Wait a minute!" he called. "What is this? What? Wait a minute!"

The ship rose, as if shedding its weight like a cloak falling to the ground, and hovered briefly. It swept strangely up into the evening sky. It passed up through the clouds, illuminating them briefly, and then was gone, leaving Arthur alone in an immensity of land dancing a helplessly tiny little dance.

"What?" he screamed. "What? What? Hey, what? Come back here and say that!"

He jumped and danced until his legs trembled, and

shouted till his lungs rasped. There was no answer from anyone. There was no one to hear him or speak to him.

The alien ship was already thundering toward the upper reaches of the atmosphere, on its way out into the appalling void that separates the very few things there are in the Universe from one another.

Its occupant, the alien with the expensive complexion, leaned back in its single seat. His name was Wowbagger the Infinitely Prolonged. He was a man with a purpose. Not a very good purpose, as he would have been the first to admit, but it was at least a purpose, and it did at least keep him on the move.

Wowbagger the Infinitely Prolonged was—indeed, is—one of the Universe's very small number of immortal beings.

Most of those who are born immortal instinctively know how to cope with it, but Wowbagger was not one of them. Indeed, he had come to hate them, the load of serene bastards. He had had his immortality inadvertently thrust upon him by an unfortunate accident with an irrational particle accelerator, a liquid lunch and a pair of rubber bands. The precise details of the accident are not important because no one has ever managed to duplicate the exact circumstances under which it happened, and many people have ended up looking very silly, or dead, or both, trying.

Wowbagger closed his eyes in a grim and weary expression, put some light jazz on the ship's stereo, and reflected that he could have made it if it hadn't been for Sunday afternoons, he really could have done.

To begin with it was fun; he had a ball, living dangerously, taking risks, cleaning up on high-yield long-term investments, and just generally outliving the hell out of everybody.

In the end, it was the Sunday afternoons he couldn't cope with, and that terrible listlessness that starts to set in at about 2:55, when you know you've taken all the baths you can usefully take that day, that however hard you stare at any given paragraph in the newspaper you will never actually read it, or use the revolutionary new pruning technique it describes, and that as you stare at the clock the hands will move relentlessly on to four o'clock, and you will enter the long dark teatime of the soul.

So things began to pall for him. The merry smiles he used to wear at other people's funerals began to fade. He began to despise the Universe in general, and everybody in it in particular.

This was the point at which he conceived his purpose, the thing that would drive him on, and which, as far as he could see, would drive him on forever. It was this.

He would insult the Universe.

That is, he would insult everybody in it. Individually, personally, one by one, and (this was the thing he really decided to grit his teeth over) in alphabetical order.

When people protested to him, as they sometimes had done, that the plan was not merely misguided but actually impossible because of the number of people being born and dying all the time, he would merely fix them with a steely look and say, "A man can dream, can't he?"

And so he had started out. He equipped a spaceship that was built to last with a computer capable of handling all the data processing involved in keeping track

5

of the entire population of the known Universe and working out the horrifically complicated routes involved.

His ship fled through the inner orbits of the Sol star system, preparing to slingshot around the sun and fling itself out into interstellar space.

"Computer," he said.

"Here," yipped the computer.

"Where next?"

"Computing that."

Wowbagger gazed for a moment at the fantastic jewelry of the night, the billions of tiny diamond worlds that dusted the infinite darkness with light. Every one, every single one was on his itinerary. Most of them he would be going to millions of times over.

He imagined for a moment his itinerary connecting all the dots in the sky like a child's numbered dots puzzle. He hoped that from some vantage point in the Universe it might be seen to spell a very, very rude word.

The computer beeped tunelessly to indicate that it had finished its calculations.

"Folfanga," it said. It beeped.

"Fourth world of the Folfanga system," it continued. It beeped again.

"Estimated journey time, three weeks," it continued further. It beeped again.

"There to meet with a small slug," it beeped, "of the genus A-Rth-Urp-Hil-Ipdenu.

"I believe," it added, after a slight pause during which it beeped, "that you had decided to call it a brainless prat."

Wowbagger grunted. He watched the majesty of creation outside his window for a moment or two.

"I think I'll take a nap," he said, and then added, "What network areas are we going to be passing through in the next few hours?"

The computer beeped.

"Cosmovid, Thinkpix and Home Brain Box," it said, and beeped.

"Any movies I haven't seen thirty thousand times already?"

"No."

"Uh."

"There's *Angst in Space*. You've only seen that thirty-three thousand five hundred and seventeen times."

"Wake me for the second reel."

The computer beeped.

"Sleep well," it said.

The ship sped on through the night.

Meanwhile, on Earth, it began to rain heavily and Arthur Dent sat in his cave and had one of the most rotten evenings of his entire life, thinking of things he could have said to the alien, and swatting flies, which also had a rotten evening.

The next day he made himself a pouch out of rabbit skin because he thought it would be useful to keep things in.

Chapter 2

This morning, two years later than that, was sweet and fragrant as he emerged from the cave he called home until he could think of a better name for it or find a better cave.

Though his throat was sore again from his early morning yell of horror, he was suddenly in a terrifically good mood. He wrapped his dilapidated dressing gown tightly around him and beamed at the bright morning. The air was clear and scented, the breeze flitted lightly through the tall grass around his cave, the birds were chirping at one another, the butterflies were flitting about prettily, and the whole of nature seemed to be conspiring to be as pleasant as it possibly could.

It wasn't all the pastoral delights that were making Arthur feel so cheery, though. He had just had a wonderful idea about how to cope with the terrible lonely isolation, the nightmares, the failure of all his attempts at horticulture, and the sheer futurelessness and futility of his life here on prehistoric Earth, which was that he would go mad.

He beamed again and took a bite out of a rabbit leg left over from his supper. He chewed happily for a few moments and then decided formally to announce his decision.

He stood up straight and looked the world squarely in the fields and hills. To add weight to his words he stuck the rabbit bone in his beard. He spread his arms out wide.

"I will go mad!" he announced.

"Good idea," said Ford Prefect, clambering down from the rock on which he had been sitting.

Arthur's brain somersaulted. His jaw did push-ups.

"I went mad for a while," said Ford, "did me no end of good."

Arthur's eyes did cartwheels.

"You see . . ." said Ford.

"Where have you been?" interrupted Arthur, now that his head had finished working out.

"Around," said Ford, "around and about." He grinned in what he accurately judged to be an infuriating manner. "I just took my mind off the hook for a bit. I reckoned that if the world wanted me badly enough it would call back. It did."

He took out of his now terribly battered and dilapidated satchel his Sub-Etha Sens-O-Matic.

"At least," he said, "I think it did. This has been playing up a bit." He shook it. "If it was a false alarm I shall go mad," he said, "again."

Arthur shook his head and sat down. He looked up.

"I thought you must be dead . . ." he said simply.

"So did I for a while," said Ford, "and then I decided I was a lemon for a couple of weeks. I kept myself amused all that time jumping in and out of a gin and tonic."

Arthur cleared his throat, and then did it again. "Where," he said, "did you . . . ?"

9

"Find a gin and tonic?" said Ford brightly. "I found a small lake that thought it was a gin and tonic, and jumped in and out of that. At least, I think it thought it was a gin and tonic.

"I may," he added with a grin that would have sent sane men scampering into trees, "have been imagining it."

He waited for a reaction from Arthur, but Arthur knew better than that.

"Carry on," he said evenly.

"The point is, you see," said Ford, "that there is no point in driving yourself mad trying to stop yourself going mad. You might just as well give in and save your sanity for later."

"And this is you sane again, is it?" asked Arthur. "I ask merely for information."

"I went to Africa," said Ford.

"Yes?"

"Yes."

"What was that like?"

"And this is your cave, is it?" said Ford.

"Er, yes," said Arthur. He felt very strange. After nearly four years of total isolation he was so pleased and relieved to see Ford that he could almost cry. Ford was, on the other hand, an almost immediately annoying person.

"Very nice," said Ford, in reference to Arthur's cave. "You must hate it."

Arthur didn't bother to reply.

"Africa was very interesting," said Ford. "I behaved very oddly there."

He gazed thoughtfully into the distance.

"I took up being cruel to animals," he said airily. "But only," he added, "as a hobby."

10

"Oh, yes," said Arthur, warily.

"Yes," Ford assured him. "I won't disturb you with the details because they would . . ."

"What?"

"Disturb you. But you may be interested to know that I am single-handedly responsible for the evolved shape of the animal you came to know in later centuries as a giraffe. And I tried to learn to fly. Do you believe me?"

"Tell me," said Arthur.

"I'll tell you later. I'll just mention that the *Guide* says . . ."

"The . . . ?"

"*Guide. The Hitchhiker's Guide to the Galaxy.* You remember?"

"Yes. I remember throwing it in the river."

"Yes," said Ford, "but I fished it out."

"You didn't tell me."

"I didn't want you to throw it in again."

"Fair enough," admitted Arthur. "It says?"

"What?"

"The *Guide* says?"

"The *Guide* says that there is an art to flying," said Ford, "or rather a knack. The knack lies in learning how to throw yourself at the ground and miss." He smiled weakly. He pointed at the knees of his trousers and held his arms up to show the elbows. They were all torn and worn through.

"I haven't done very well so far," he said. He stuck out his hand. "I'm very glad to see you again, Arthur," he added.

Arthur shook his head in a sudden access of emotion and bewilderment.

"I haven't seen anyone for years," he said, "not

anyone. I can hardly even remember how to speak. I keep forgetting words. I practice, you see. I practice by talking to . . . talking to . . . what are those things people think you're mad if you talk to? Like George the Third."

"Kings?" suggested Ford.

"No, no," said Arthur, "the things he used to talk to. We're surrounded by them, for heaven's sake. I've planted hundreds myself. They all died. Trees! I practice by talking to trees. What's that for?"

Ford still had his hand stuck out. Arthur looked at it with incomprehension.

"Shake," prompted Ford.

Arthur did, nervously at first, as if it might turn out to be a fish. Then he grasped it vigorously with both hands in an overwhelming flood of relief. He shook it and shook it.

After a while Ford found it necessary to disengage. They climbed to the top of a nearby outcrop of rock and surveyed the scene around them.

"What happened to the Golgafrinchans?" asked Ford.

Arthur shrugged.

"A lot of them didn't make it through the winter three years ago," he said, "and the few who remained in the spring said they needed a holiday and set off on a raft. History says that they must have survived. . . ."

"Huh," said Ford, "well well." He stuck his hands on his hips and looked around again at the empty world. Suddenly, there was about Ford a sense of energy and purpose.

"We're going," he said excitedly, and shivered with energy.

"Where? How?" said Arthur.

"I don't know," said Ford, "but I just feel that the time is right. Things are going to happen. We're on our way."

He lowered his voice to a whisper.

"I have detected," he said, "disturbances in the wash."

He gazed keenly into the distance and looked as if he would quite like the wind to blow his hair back dramatically at that point, but the wind was busy fooling around with some leaves a little way off.

Arthur asked him to repeat what he had just said because he hadn't quite understood his meaning. Ford repeated it.

"The wash?" said Arthur.

"The space-time wash," said Ford and, as the wind blew briefly past at that moment, he bared his teeth into it.

Arthur nodded, and then cleared his throat.

"Are we talking about," he asked cautiously, "some sort of Vogon laundromat, or what are we talking about?"

"Eddies," said Ford, "in the space-time continuum."

"Ah," nodded Arthur, "is he. Is he." He pushed his hands into the pockets of his dressing gown and looked knowledgeably into the distance.

"What?" said Ford.

"Er, who," said Arthur, "is Eddy, then, exactly, then?"

Ford looked angrily at him.

"Will you listen?" he snapped.

"I have been listening," said Arthur, "but I'm not sure it's helped."

Ford grasped him by the lapels of his dressing gown and spoke to him as slowly and distinctly and

13

patiently as if he were somebody from the telephone company accounts department.

"There seem . . ." he said, "to be some pools . . ." he said, "of instability . . ." he said, "in the fabric . . ." he said. . . .

Arthur looked foolishly at the cloth of his dressing gown where Ford was holding it. Ford swept on before Arthur could turn the foolish look into a foolish remark.

". . . in the fabric of space-time," he said.

"Ah, that," said Arthur.

"Yes, that," confirmed Ford.

They stood there alone on a hill on prehistoric Earth and stared each other resolutely in the face.

"And it's done what?" said Arthur.

"It," said Ford, "has developed pools of instability."

"Has it," said Arthur, his eyes not wavering for a moment.

"It has," said Ford, with a similar degree of ocular immobility.

"Good," said Arthur.

"See?" said Ford.

"No," said Arthur.

There was a quiet pause.

"The difficulty with this conversation," said Arthur after a sort of ponderous look had crawled slowly across his face like a mountaineer negotiating a tricky outcrop, "is that it's very different from most of the ones I've had of late. Which, as I explained, have mostly been with trees. They weren't like this. Except perhaps some of the ones I've had with elms that sometimes got a bit bogged down."

"Arthur," said Ford.

14

"Hello? Yes?" said Arthur.

"Just believe everything I tell you, and it will all be very, very simple."

"Ah, well, I'm not sure I believe that."

They sat down and composed their thoughts.

Ford got out his Sub-Etha Sens-O-Matic. It was making vague humming noises and a tiny light on it was flickering faintly.

"Flat battery?" said Arthur.

"No," said Ford, "there is a moving disturbance in the fabric of space-time, an eddy, a pool of instability, and it's somewhere in our vicinity."

"Where?"

Ford moved the device in a slow, lightly bobbing semicircle. Suddenly the light flashed.

"There!" said Ford, shooting out his arm; "there, behind that sofa!"

Arthur looked. Much to his surprise, there was a velvet paisley–covered Chesterfield sofa in the field in front of them. He boggled intelligently at it. Shrewd questions sprang into his mind.

"Why," he said, "is there a sofa in that field?"

"I told you!" shouted Ford, leaping to his feet. "Eddies in the space-time continuum!"

"And this is his sofa, is it?" asked Arthur, struggling to his feet and, he hoped, though not very optimistically, to his senses.

"Arthur!" shouted Ford at him, "that sofa is there because of the space-time instability I've been trying to get your terminally softened brain to come to grips with. It's been washed up out of the continuum, it's space-time jetsam, it doesn't matter what it is, we've got to catch it, it's our only way out of here!"

He scrambled rapidly down the rocky outcrop and made off across the field.

"Catch it?" muttered Arthur, then frowned in bemusement as he saw that the Chesterfield was lazily bobbing and wafting away across the grass.

With a whoop of utterly unexpected delight he leaped down the rock and plunged off in hectic pursuit of Ford Prefect and the irrational piece of furniture.

They careened wildly through the grass, leaping, laughing, shouting instructions to each other to head the thing off this way or that way. The sun shone dreamily on the swaying grass, tiny field animals scattered crazily in their wake.

Arthur felt happy. He was terribly pleased that the day was for once working out so much according to plan. Only twenty minutes ago he had decided he would go mad, and now here he was already chasing a Chesterfield sofa across the fields of prehistoric Earth.

The sofa bobbed this way and that and seemed simultaneously to be as solid as the trees as it drifted past some of them and hazy as a billowing dream as it floated like a ghost through others.

Ford and Arthur pounded chaotically after it, but it dodged and weaved as if following its own complex mathematical topography, which it was. Still they pursued, still it danced and spun, and suddenly turned and dipped as if crossing the lip of a catastrophe graph, and they were practically on top of it. With a heave and a shout they leaped on it, the sun winked out, they fell through a sickening nothingness and emerged unexpectedly in the middle of the pitch at Lord's Cricket Ground, St. John's Wood, London, toward the end of the last Test Match of the Australian series in the year 198—, with England only needing twenty-eight runs to win.

Important Fact from Galactic History, Number One:
(reproduced from the Siderial Daily Mentioner's Book of Popular Galactic History)

The night sky over the planet Krikkit is the least interesting sight in the entire Universe.

Chapter 3

It was a charming and delightful day at Lord's as Ford and Arthur tumbled haphazardly out of a space-time anomaly and hit the immaculate turf rather hard.

The applause of the crowd was tremendous. It wasn't for them, but instinctively they bowed anyway, which was fortunate because the small red heavy ball that the crowd actually had been applauding whistled mere inches over Arthur's head. They threw themselves back to the ground that seemed to spin hideously around them.

"What was that?" hissed Arthur.

"Something red," hissed Ford back at him.

"Where are we?"

"Er, somewhere green."

"Shapes," muttered Arthur, "I need shapes."

The applause of the crowd had been rapidly succeeded by gasps of astonishment, and the awkward titters of hundreds of people who could not yet make up their minds whether to believe what they had just seen or not.

"This your sofa?" said a voice.

"What was that?" whispered Ford.

Arthur looked up.

"Something blue," he said.

"Shape?" asked Ford.

Arthur looked again.

"It is shaped," he hissed at Ford, with his brow savagely furrowed, "like a policeman."

They remained crouched there for a few moments, frowning deeply. The blue thing shaped like a policeman tapped them both on the shoulders.

"Come on, you two," the shape said, "let's go."

These words had an electrifying effect on Arthur. He leaped to his feet and shot a series of startled glances at the panorama around him that had suddenly settled down into something of quite terrifying ordinariness.

"Where did you get this from?" he yelled at the policeman shape.

"What did you say?" said the startled shape.

"This is Lord's Cricket Ground, isn't it?" snapped Arthur. "Where did you find it, how did you get it here? I think," he added, clasping his hand to his brow, "that I had better calm down." He squatted down abruptly in front of Ford.

"It is a policeman," he said. "What do we do?"

Ford shrugged. "What do you want to do?" he said.

"I want you," said Arthur, "to tell me that I have been dreaming for the last five years."

Ford shrugged again, and obliged.

"You've been dreaming for the last five years," he said.

Arthur got to his feet.

"It's all right, officer," he said, "I've been dreaming for the last five years. Ask him," he added, pointing at Ford, "he was in it." Having said this, he sauntered off toward the edge of the pitch, brushing down his dressing gown. He then noticed his dressing gown and stopped. He stared at it. He turned around. He flung himself at the policeman.

"So where did I get these clothes from?" he howled.

He collapsed and lay twitching on the grass.

Ford shook his head.

"He's had a bad two million years," he said to the policeman, and together they heaved Arthur onto the sofa and carried him off the pitch and were only briefly hampered by the sudden disappearance of the sofa on the way.

Reactions to all this from the crowd were many and various. Most of them couldn't cope with watching it, and listened to it on the radio instead.

"Well, this is an interesting incident, Brian," said one radio commentator to another. "I don't think there have been any mysterious materializations on the pitch since, oh, since, well, I don't think there have been any, have there? That I recall?"

"Edgbaston 1932?"

"Ah, now what happened then . . . ?"

"Well, Peter, I think it was Canter facing Willcox coming up to bowl from the pavilion end when a spectator suddenly ran straight across the pitch."

There was a pause while the first commentator considered this.

"Ye . . . e . . . s . . ." he said, "yes, there's nothing actually very mysterious about that, is there? He didn't actually materialize, did he? Just ran on."

"No, that's true, but he did claim to have *seen* something materialize on the pitch."

"Ah, did he."

"Yes. An alligator, I think, of some description."

"And what happened to the man?"

"Well, I think someone offered to take him off and give him some lunch, but he explained that he'd already had a rather good one, so the matter was dropped and Warwickshire went on to win by three wickets."

"So, not very like this current instance. For those of you who've just tuned in, you may be interested to know that, er . . . two men, two rather scruffily attired men, and indeed a sofa—a Chesterfield I think?"

"Yes, a Chesterfield."

"Have just materialized here in the middle of Lord's Cricket Ground. But I don't think they meant any harm, they've been very good-natured about it, and . . ."

"Sorry, can I interrupt you a moment, Peter, and say that the sofa has just vanished."

"So it has. Well, that's one mystery less. Still, it's definitely one for the record books I think, particularly occurring at this dramatic moment in play, England now needing only twenty-four runs to win the series. The men are leaving the pitch in the company of a police officer, and I think everyone's settling down now and play is about to resume."

"Now, sir," said the policeman after they had made a passage through the curious crowd and laid Arthur's peacefully inert body on a blanket, "perhaps you'd care to tell me who you are, where you come from and what that little scene was all about?"

Ford looked at the ground for a moment as if steadying himself for something, then he straightened up and aimed a look at the policeman that hit him with the full force of every inch of the six light-years' distance between Earth and Ford's home near Betelgeuse.

22

"All right," said Ford, very quietly, "I'll tell you."

"Yes, well, that won't be necessary," said the policeman hurriedly, "just don't let whatever it was happen again." The policeman turned around and wandered off in search of anyone who wasn't from Betelgeuse. Fortunately, the cricket ground was full of them.

Arthur's consciousness approached his body as from a great distance, and reluctantly. It had had some bad times in there. Slowly, nervously, it entered and settled down into its accustomed position.

Arthur sat up.

"Where am I?" he said.

"Lord's Cricket Ground," said Ford.

"Fine," said Arthur, and his consciousness stepped out again for a quick breather. His body flopped back on the grass.

Ten minutes later, hunched over a cup of tea in the refreshment tent, the color started to come back to his haggard face.

"How you feeling?" asked Ford.

"I'm home," said Arthur hoarsely. He closed his eyes and greedily inhaled the steam from his tea as if it were—well, as far as Arthur was concerned, as if it were tea, which it was.

"I'm home," he repeated, "home. It's England, it's today, the nightmare is over." He opened his eyes again and smiled serenly. "I'm where I belong," he said in an emotional whisper.

"There are two things I feel I should tell you," said Ford, tossing a copy of the *Guardian* over the table at him.

"I'm home," said Arthur.

"Yes," said Ford. "One is," he said, pointing at the

23

date at the top of the paper, "that the Earth will be demolished in two days' time."

"I'm home," said Arthur, "tea," he said, "cricket," he added, with pleasure, "mown grass, wooden benches, white linen jackets, beer cans. . . ."

Slowly he began to focus on the newspaper. He cocked his head on one side with a slight frown.

"I've seen that one before," he said. His eyes wandered slowly up to the date, which Ford was idly tapping at. His face froze for a second or two and then began to do that terribly slow crashing trick that Arctic ice floes do so spectacularly in the spring.

"And the other thing," said Ford, "is that you appear to have a bone in your beard." He tossed back his tea.

Outside the refreshment tent, the sun was shining on a happy crowd. It shone on white hats and red faces. It shone on Popsicles and melted them. It shone on the tears of small children whose Popsicles had just melted and fallen off the stick. It shone on the trees, it flashed off whirling cricket bats, it gleamed off the utterly extraodinary object that was parked behind the sight screens and that nobody appeared to have noticed. It beamed on Ford and Arthur as they emerged blinking from the refreshment tent and surveyed the scene around them.

Arthur was shaking.

"Perhaps," he said, "I should . . ."

"No," said Ford, sharply.

"What?" said Arthur.

"Don't try and phone yourself up at home."

"How did you know . . . ?"

Ford shrugged.

"But why not?" said Arthur.

"People who talk to themselves on the phone," said Ford, "never learn anything to their advantage."

"But . . ."

"Look," said Ford. He picked up an imaginary phone and dialed an imaginary dial.

"Hello?" he said into the imaginary mouthpiece. "Is that Aurthur Dent? Ah, hello, yes. This is Arthur Dent speaking. Don't hang up."

He looked at the imaginary phone in disappointment.

"He hung up," he said, shrugged and put the imaginary phone neatly back on its imaginary hook.

"This is not my first temporal anomaly," he added.

A glummer look replaced the already glum look on Arthur Dent's face.

"So we're not home and dry," he said.

"We could not even be said," replied Ford, "to be home and vigorously toweling ourselves off."

The cricket game continued. The bowler approached the wicket at a lope, a trot and then a run. He suddenly exploded in a flurry of arms and legs, out of which flew a ball. The batsman swung and thwacked it behind him over the sight screens. Ford's eyes followed the trajectory of the ball and jogged momentarily. He stiffened. He looked along the flight path of the ball again and his eyes twitched again.

"This isn't my towel," said Arthur, who was rummaging in his rabbit-skin bag.

"Shhh," said Ford. He screwed his eyes up in concentration.

"I had a Golgafrinchan jogging towel," continued Arthur; "it was blue with yellow stars on it. This isn't it."

"Shhh," said Ford again. He covered one eye and looked with the other.

"This one's pink," said Arthur. "It isn't yours, is it?"

"I would like you to shut up about your towel," said Ford.

"It isn't my towel," insisted Arthur, "that is the point I am trying to . . ."

"And the time at which I would like you to shut up about it," continued Ford in a low growl, "is now."

"All right," said Arthur, starting to stuff it back into the primitively stitched rabbit-skin bag. "I realize that it is probably not important in the cosmic scale of things, it's just odd, that's all. A pink towel suddenly, instead of a blue one with yellow stars."

Ford was beginning to behave rather strangely, or rather not actually beginning to behave strangely but beginning to behave in a way that was strangely different from the other strange ways in which he more regularly behaved. What he was doing was this. Regardless of the bemused stares it was provoking from his fellow members of the crowd gathered round the pitch, he was waving his hands in sharp movements across his face, ducking down behind some people, leaping up behind others, then standing still and blinking a lot. After a moment or two of this he started to stalk forward slowly and stealthily, wearing a puzzled frown of concentration, like a leopard that is not sure whether it's just seen a half-empty tin of cat food half a mile away across a hot and dusty plain.

"This isn't my bag either," said Arthur suddenly.

Ford's spell of concentration was broken. He turned angrily on Arthur.

"I wasn't talking about my towel," said Arthur.

"We've established that it isn't mine. It's just that the bag into which I was putting the towel that is not mine is also not mine, though it is extraordinarily similar. Now personally, I think that that is extremely odd, especially as the bag was one I made myself on prehistoric Earth. These are also not my stones," he added, pulling a few flat gray stones out of the bag. "I was making a collection of interesting stones and these are clearly very dull ones."

A roar of excitement thrilled through the crowd and obliterated whatever it was that Ford said in reply to this piece of information. The cricket ball that had excited this reaction fell out of the sky and dropped neatly into Arthur's mysterious rabbit-skin bag.

"Now I would say that that was also a very curious event," said Arthur, rapidly closing the bag and pretending to look for the ball on the ground.

"I don't think it's here," he said to the small boys who immediately clustered around him to join in the search; "it probably rolled off somewhere. Over there I expect." He pointed vaguely in the direction in which he wished they would push off. One of the boys looked at him quizzically.

"You all right?" said the boy.

"No," said Arthur.

"That why you got a bone in your beard?" said the boy.

"I'm training it to like being wherever it's put." Arthur prided himself on saying this. It was, he thought, exactly the sort of thing that would entertain and stimulate young minds.

"Oh," said the small boy, putting his head on the one side and thinking about it. "What's your name?"

"Dent," said Arthur, "Arthur Dent."

"You're a jerk, Dent," said the boy, "a complete kneebiter." The boy looked past him at something else, to show that he wasn't in any particular hurry to run away, and then wandered off scratching his nose. Suddenly Arthur remembered that the Earth was going to be demolished again in two days' time, and just this once didn't feel too bad about it. Play resumed with a new ball, the sun continued to shine and Ford continued to jump up and down shaking his head and blinking.

"Something's on your mind, isn't it?" said Arthur.

"I think," said Ford in a tone of voice that Arthur by now recognized as one that presaged something utterly unintelligible, "that there's an S.E.P. over there."

He pointed. Curiously enough, the direction he pointed in was not the one in which he was looking. Arthur looked in the one direction, which was toward the sight screens, and in the other, which was at the field of play. He nodded, he shrugged. He shrugged again.

"A what?" he said.

"An S.E.P."

"An S . . . ?"

". . . E.P."

"And what's that?"

"Somebody Else's Problem," said Ford.

"Ah, good," said Arthur, and relaxed. He had no idea what all that was about, but at least it seemed to be over. It wasn't.

"Over there," said Ford, again pointing at the sight screens and looking at the pitch.

"Where?" said Arthur.

"There!" said Ford.

"I see," said Arthur, who didn't.

28

"You do?" said Ford.

"What?" said Arthur.

"Can you see," said Ford patiently, "the S.E.P.?"

"I thought you said that was someone else's problem."

"That's right."

Arthur nodded slowly, carefully and with an air of immense stupidity.

"And I want to know," said Ford, "if you can see it."

"You do?"

"Yes!"

"What," said Arthur, "does it look like?"

"Well, how should I know, you fool," shouted Ford. "If you can see it, you tell me."

Arthur experienced that dull throbbing sensation just behind the temples that was a hallmark of so many of his conversations with Ford. His brain lurked like a frightened puppy in its kennel. Ford took him by the arm.

"An S.E.P.," he said, "is something that we can't see, or don't see, or our brain doesn't let us see, because we think that it's somebody else's problem. That's what S.E.P. means. Somebody Else's Problem. The brain just edits it out; it's like a blind spot. If you look at it directly you won't see it unless you know precisely what it is. Your only hope is to catch it by surprise out of the corner of your eye."

"Ah," said Arthur, "then that's why . . ."

"Yes," said Ford, who knew what Arthur was going to say.

". . . you've been jumping up and . . ."

"Yes."

". . . down, and blinking . . ."

"Yes."

". . . and . . ."

"I think you've got the message."

"I can see it," said Arthur, "it's a spaceship."

For a moment Arthur was stunned by the reaction this revelation provoked. A roar erupted from the crowd, and from every direction people were running and shouting, yelling, tumbling over one another in a tumult of confusion. He stumbled back in astonishment and glanced fearfully around. Then he glanced around again in even greater astonishment.

"Exciting, isn't it?" said an apparition. The apparition wobbled in front of Arthur's eyes, though the truth of the matter is probably that Arthur's eyes were wobbling in front of the apparition. His mouth wobbled as well.

"W . . . w . . . w . . . w . . ." his mouth said.

"I think your team has just won," said the apparition.

"W . . . w . . . w . . . w . . ." repeated Arthur, and punctuated each wobble with a prod at Ford Prefect's back. Ford was staring at the tumult in trepidation.

"You are English, aren't you?" said the apparition.

"W . . . w . . . w . . . w . . . yes," said Arthur.

"Well, your team, as I say, has just won. The match. It means they retain the Ashes. You must be very pleased. I must say, I'm rather fond of cricket, though I wouldn't like anyone outside this planet to hear me saying that. Oh dear no."

The apparition gave what might have been a mischievous grin, but it was hard to tell because the sun was directly behind him, creating a blinding halo around his head and illuminating his silver hair and beard in a way that was awesome, dramatic and hard to reconcile with mischievous grins.

"Still," he said, "it'll all be over in a couple of days, won't it? Though as I said to you when we last met, I was very sorry about that. Still, whatever will have been, will have been."

Arthur tried to speak, but gave up the unequal struggle. He prodded Ford again.

"I thought something terrible had happened," said Ford, "but it's just the end of the game. We ought to get out. Oh, hello, Slartibartfast, what are you doing here?"

"Oh, pottering, pottering," said the old man gravely.

"That your ship? Can you give us a lift anywhere?"

"Patience, patience," the old man admonished.

"Okay," said Ford, "it's just that this planet's going to be demolished pretty soon."

"I know that," said Slartibartfast.

"And, well, I just wanted to make that point," said Ford.

"The point is taken."

"And if you feel that you really want to hang around a cricket pitch at this point . . ."

"I do."

"Then, it's your ship."

"It is."

"I suppose." Ford turned away sharply at this point.

"Hello, Slartibartfast," said Arthur at last.

"Hello, Earthman," said Slartibartfast.

"After all," said Ford, "we can only die once."

The old man ignored this and stared keenly onto the pitch, with eyes that seemed alive with expressions that had no apparent bearing on what was happening out there. What was happening was that the crowd was gathering itself into a wide circle around the center of the pitch. What Slartibartfast saw in it, he alone knew.

Ford was humming something. It was just one note repeated at intervals. He was hoping that somebody would ask him what he was humming, but nobody did. If anybody had asked him he would have said he was humming the first line of a Noël Coward song called "Mad About the Boy" over and over again. It would then have been pointed out to him that he was only singing one note, to which he would have replied that for reasons that he hoped would be apparent, he was omitting the "about the boy" bit. He was annoyed that nobody asked.

"It's just," he burst out at last, "that if we don't go soon, we might get caught in the middle of it all again. And there's nothing that depresses me more than seeing a planet being destroyed. Except possibly still being on it when it happens. Or," he added in an undertone, "hanging around cricket matches."

"Patience," said Slartibartfast again, "great things are afoot."

"That's what you said last time we met," said Arthur.

"They were," said Slartibartfast.

"Yes, that's true," admitted Arthur.

All, however, that seemed to be afoot was a ceremony of some kind. It was being specially staged for the benefit of television rather than the spectators, and all they could gather about it from where they were standing was what they heard from a nearby radio. Ford was aggressively uninterested.

He fretted as he heard it explained that the Ashes were about to be presented to the captain of the English team out there on the pitch, fumed when told that this was because they had now won it for the *nth* time, positively barked with annoyance at the information that the Ashes were the remains of a cricket stump, and when, further to this, he was asked to contend with the fact that the cricket stump in question had been burnt in Melbourne, Australia, in 1882, to signify the "death of English cricket," he rounded on Slartibartfast, took a deep breath, but didn't have a chance to say anything because the old man wasn't there. He was marching out onto the pitch with terrible purpose in his gait; his hair, beard and robes swept behind him, looking very much as Moses would have looked if Sinai had been a well-cut lawn instead of, as it is more usually represented, a fiery smoking mountain.

"He said to meet him at his ship," said Arthur.

"What in the name of zarking fardwarks is the old fool doing?" exploded Ford.

"Meeting us at his ship in two minutes," said Arthur with a shrug which indicated total abdication of thought. They started off toward it. Strange sounds reached their ears. They tried not to listen, but could not help noticing that Slartibartfast was querulously demanding that he be given the silver urn containing the Ashes, as they were, he said, "vitally important for the past, present and future safety of the Galaxy," and that this was causing wild hilarity. They resolved to ignore it.

What happened next they could not ignore. With a noise like a hundred thousand people saying "whop," a steely white spaceship suddenly seemed to create itself out of nothing in the air directly above the cricket pitch and hung there with infinite menace and a slight hum.

Then for a while it did nothing, as if it expected everybody to go about their normal business and not mind its just hanging there.

Then it did something quite extraordinary. Or rather, it opened up and let something quite extraordinary come out of it, eleven quite extraordinary things.

They were robots, white robots.

What was most extraordinary about them was that they appeared to have come dressed for the occasion. Not only were they white, but they carried what appeared to be cricket bats, and not only that but they also carried what appeared to be cricket balls, and not only that but they wore white ribbing pads around the lower parts of their legs. These last were extraordinary because they appeared to contain jets that allowed these curiously civilized robots to fly down from their hovering spaceship and start to kill people, which is what they did.

"Hello," said Arthur, "something seems to be happening."

"Get to the ship," shouted Ford. "I don't want to know, just get to the ship." He started to run. "I don't want to know, I don't want to see, I don't want to hear," he yelled as he ran, "this is not my planet, I didn't choose to be here, I don't want to get involved, just get me out of here, and get me to a party with people I can relate to!"

Smoke and flame billowed from the pitch.

"Well, the supernatural brigade certainly seems to be out in force here today . . ." burbled a radio happily to itself.

"What I need," shouted Ford, by way of clarifying

his previous remarks, "is a strong drink and a peer group." He continued to run, pausing only for a moment to grab Arthur's arm and drag him along with him. Arthur had adopted his normal crisis role, which was to stand with his mouth hanging open and let it all wash over him.

"They're playing cricket," muttered Arthur, stumbling along after Ford. "I swear they are playing cricket. I do not know why they are doing this, but that is what they are doing. They're not just killing people, they're sending them up," he shouted. "Ford, they're sending us up!"

It would have been hard to disbelieve this without knowing a great deal more Galactic history than Arthur had so far managed to pick up in his travels. The ghostly but violent shapes that could be seen moving within the thick pall of smoke seemed to be performing a series of bizarre parodies of batting strokes, the difference being that every ball they struck with their bats exploded wherever it landed. The very first one of these had dispelled Arthur's initial reaction that the whole thing might just be a publicity stunt by Australian margarine manufacturers.

And then, as suddenly as it had all started, it was over. The eleven white robots ascended through the seething cloud in a tight formation, and with a few last flashes of flame entered the bowels of their hovering white ship, which, with a noise like a hundred thousand people saying "foop," promptly vanished into the thin air out of which it had whopped.

For a moment there was a terrible stunned silence, and then out of the drifting smoke emerged the pale figure of Slartibartfast looking even more like Moses because in spite of the continued absence of the mountain he was at least now striding across a fiery and smoking well-mown lawn.

He stared wildly about him until he saw the hurrying figures of Arthur Dent and Ford Prefect forcing their way through the frightened crowd that was for the moment busy stampeding in the opposite direction. The crowd was clearly thinking to itself what an unusual day this was turning out to be, and not really knowing which way, if any, to turn.

Slartibartfast was gesticulating urgently at Ford and Arthur and shouting at them, as the three gradually converged on his ship, still parked behind the sight screens and still apparently unnoticed by the crowd stampeding past it who presumably had enough of their own problems to cope with at that time.

"They've garble warble farble!" shouted Slartibartfast in his thin tremulous voice.

"What did he say?" panted Ford, as he elbowed his way onward.

Arthur shook his head.

"They've . . . something or other," he said.

"They've table warble farble!" shouted Slartibartfast again.

Ford and Arthur shook their heads at each other.

"It sounds urgent," Arthur said. He stopped and shouted. "What?"

"They've garble warble fashes!" cried Slartibartfast, still waving at them.

"He says," said Arthur, "that they've taken the Ashes. That is what I think he is saying." They ran on.

"The . . . ?" said Ford.

"Ashes," said Arthur tersely. "The burnt remains of a cricket stump. It's a trophy. That . . ." he was panting, "is . . . apparently . . . what they . . . have come

36

and taken." He shook his head very slightly as if he were trying to get his brain to settle down lower in his skull.

"Strange thing to want to tell us," snapped Ford.

"Strange thing to take."

"Strange ship."

They had arrived at it. The second strangest thing about the ship was watching the Somebody Else's Problem field at work. They could now clearly see the ship for what it was simply because they knew it was there. It was quite apparent, however, that nobody else could. This wasn't because it was actually invisible or anything hyperimpossible like that. The technology involved in making anything invisible is so infinitely complex that nine hundred and ninety-nine billion, nine hundred and ninety-nine million, nine hundred and ninety-nine thousand, nine hundred and ninety-nine times out of a trillion it is much simpler and more effective just to take the thing away and do without it. The ultrafamous sciento-magician Effrafax of Wug once bet his life that, given a year, he could render the great megamountain Magramal entirely invisible.

Having spent most of the year jiggling around with immense Lux-O-Valves and Refracto-Nullifiers and Spectrum-By-Pass-O-Matics, he realized, with nine hours to go, that he wasn't going to make it.

So, he and his friends, and his friends' friends, and his friends' friends' friends, and his friends' friends' friends' friends, and some rather less good friends of theirs who happened to own a major stellar trucking company, put in what is now widely recognized as being the hardest night's work in history and, sure enough, on the following day, Magramal was no longer visible. Effrafax lost his bet—and therefore his life—simply because some pedantic adjudicating official noticed (a) that when walking around the area where Magramal ought to be he didn't trip over or break his nose on anything, and (b) a suspicious-looking extra moon.

The Somebody Else's Problem field is much simpler and more effective, and what is more can be run for over a hundred years on a single flashlight battery. This is because it relies on people's natural predisposition not to see anything they don't want to, weren't expecting or can't explain. If Effrafax had painted the mountain pink and erected a cheap and simple Somebody Else's Problem field on it, then people would have walked past the mountain, around it, even over it, and simply never have noticed that the thing was there.

And this is precisely what was happening with Slartibartfast's ship. It wasn't pink, but if it had been, that would have been the least of its visual problems and people were simply ignoring it like anything.

The most extraordinary thing about it was that it looked only partly like a spaceship with guidance fins, rocket engines and escape hatches and so on, and a great deal like a small, upended Italian bistro.

Ford and Arthur gazed up at it with wonderment and deeply offended sensibilities.

"Yes, I know," said Slartibartfast, hurrying up to them at that point, breathless and agitated, "but there is a reason. Come, we must go. The ancient nightmare is come again. Doom confronts us all. We must leave at once."

"I fancy somewhere sunny," said Ford.

Ford and Arthur followed Slartibartfast into the ship

38

and were so perplexed by what they saw inside it that they were totally unaware of what happened next outside.

A spaceship, yet another one, but this one sleek and silver, descended from the sky onto the pitch, quietly, without fuss, its long legs unlocking in a smooth ballet of technology.

It landed gently. It extended a short ramp. A tall gray green figure marched briskly out and approached the small knot of people who were gathered in the center of the pitch tending to the casualties of the recent bizarre massacre. It moved people aside with quiet understated authority, and came at last to a man lying in a desperate pool of blood, clearly now beyond the reach of any earthly medicine, breathing, coughing his last. The figure knelt down quietly beside him.

"Arthur Philip Deodat?" asked the figure.

The man, with horrified confusion in his eyes, nodded feebly.

"You're a no-good dumbo nothing," whispered the creature. "I thought you should know that before you went."

Chapter 4

It seemed to Arthur as if the whole sky suddenly just stood aside and let them through.

It seemed to him that the atoms of his brain and the atoms of the cosmos were streaming through each other.

It seemed to him that he was blown on the wind of the Universe, and that the wind was him.

It seemed to him that he was one of the thoughts of the Universe and that the Universe was a thought of his.

It seemed to the people at Lord's Cricket Ground that another north London restaurant had just come and gone as they so often do, and that this was Somebody Else's Problem.

"What happened?" whispered Arthur in considerable awe.

"We took off," said Slartibartfast.

Arthur lay in startled stillness on the acceleration couch. He wasn't certain whether he had just got space-sickness or religion.

"Nice mover," said Ford in an unsuccessful attempt to disguise the degree to which he had been impressed by what Slartibartfast's ship had just done. "Shame about the decor."

For a moment or two the old man didn't reply. He was staring at the instruments with the air of one who is trying to convert Fahrenheit to centigrade in his head while his house is burning down. Then his brow cleared and he stared for a moment at the wide panoramic screen in front of him, which displayed a bewildering complexity of stars streaming like silver threads around them. His lips moved as if he were trying to spell something. Suddenly his eyes darted in alarm back to his instruments, but then his expression merely subsided into a steady frown. He looked back up at the screen. He felt his own pulse. His frown deepened for a moment, then he relaxed.

"It's a mistake to try to understand machines," he said, "they only worry me. What did you say?"

"Decor," said Ford, "pity about it."

"Deep in the fundamental heart of mind and Universe," said Slartibartfast, "there is a reason."

Ford glanced sharply around. He clearly thought this was taking an optimistic view of things.

The interior of the flight deck was dark green, dark red, dark brown, cramped and moodily lit. Inexplicably, the resemblance to a small Italian bistro had failed to end at the hatchway. Small pools of light picked out pot plants, glazed tiles and all sorts of little unidentifiable brass things.

Raffia-wrapped bottles lurked hideously in the shadows.

The instruments that had occupied Slartibartfast's attention seemed to be mounted in the bottoms of bottles that were set in concrete.

Ford reached out and touched it.

Fake concrete. Plastic. Fake bottles set in fake concrete.

The fundamental heart of mind and Universe can take a running jump, he thought to himself, this is rubbish. On the other hand, it could not be denied that the way the ship had moved made the *Heart of Gold* seem like an electric pram.

He swung himself off the couch. He brushed himself off. He looked at Arthur, who was singing quietly to himself. He looked at the screen and recognized nothing. He looked at Slartibartfast.

"How far did we just travel?" he said.

"About . . ." said Slartibartfast, "about two-thirds of the way across the Galactic disc, I would say, roughly. Yes, roughly two-thirds, I think."

"It's a strange thing," said Arthur quietly, "that the farther and faster one travels across the Universe, the more one's position in it seems to be largely immaterial, and one is filled with a profound, or rather emptied of a . . ."

"Yes, very strange," said Ford. "Where are we going?"

"We are going," said Slartibartfast, "to confront an ancient nightmare of the Universe."

"And where are you going to drop us off?"

"I will need your help."

"Tough. Look, there's somewhere you can take us where we can have fun, I'm trying to think of it; we can get drunk and maybe listen to some extremely evil music. Hold on, I'll look it up." He dug out his copy of *The Hitchhiker's Guide to the Galaxy* and zipped through those parts of the index primarily concerned with sex, drugs and rock 'n' roll.

"A curse has arisen from the mists of time," said Slartibartfast.

"Yes, I expect so," said Ford. "Hey," he said, light-

42

ing accidentally on one particular reference entry, "Eccentrica Gallumbits, did you ever meet her? The triple-breasted whore of Eroticon Six. Some people say her erogenous zones start some four miles from her actual body. Me, I disagree, I say five."

"A curse," said Slartibartfast, "which will engulf the Galaxy in fire and destruction, and possibly bring the Universe to a premature doom. I mean it," he added.

"Sounds like a bad time," said Ford; "with luck I'll be drunk enough not to notice. Here," he said, stabbing his finger at the screen of the *Guide*, "would be a really wicked place to go, and I think we should. What do you say, Arthur? Stop mumbling mantras and pay attention. There's important stuff you're missing here."

Arthur pushed himself up from his couch and shook his head.

"Where are we going?" he said.

"To confront an ancient night—"

"Can it," said Ford. "Arthur, we are going out into the Galaxy to have some fun. Is that an idea you can cope with?"

"What's Slartibartfast looking so anxious about?" said Arthur.

"Nothing," said Ford.

"Doom," said Slartibartfast. "Come," he added, with sudden authority, "there is much I must show and tell you."

He walked toward a green wrought-iron spiral staircase set incomprehensibly in the middle of the flight deck and started to ascend. Arthur, with a frown, followed.

Ford slung the *Guide* sullenly back into his satchel.

"My doctor says that I have a malformed public duty gland and a natural deficiency in moral fiber," he muttered to himself, "and that I am therefore excused from saving Universes."

Nevertheless, he stomped up the stairs behind them.

What they found upstairs was just stupid, or so it seemed, and Ford shook his head, buried his face in his hands and slumped against a pot plant, crushing it against the wall.

"The central computational area," said Slartibartfast, unperturbed. "This is where every calculation affecting the ship in any way is performed. Yes, I know what it looks like, but it is in fact a complex four-dimensional topographical map of a series of highly complex mathematical functions."

"It looks like a joke," said Arthur.

"I know what it looks like," said Slartibartfast, and went into it. As he did so, Arthur had a sudden vague flash of what it might mean, but he refused to believe it. The Universe could not possibly work like that, he thought, cannot possibly. That, he thought to himself, would be as absurd as, as absurd as . . . he terminated that line of thinking. Most of the absurd things he could think of had already happened.

And this was one of them.

It was a large glass cage, or box—in fact a room.

In it was a table, a long one. Around it were gathered about a dozen chairs, of the bentwood style. On it was a tablecloth—a grubby, red-and-white check tablecloth, scarred with the occasional cigarette burn, each, presumably, at a precisely calculated mathematical position.

And on the tablecloth sat some dozen half-eaten Italian meals, hedged about with half-eaten breadsticks

44

and half-drunk glasses of wine, and toyed with list-lessly by robots.

It was all completely artificial. The robot customers were attended by a robot waiter, a robot wine waiter and a robot maître d'. The furniture was artificial, the tablecloth artificial and each particular piece of food was clearly capable of exhibiting all the mechanical characteristics of, say, a *pollo sorpreso*, without actually being one.

And all participated in a little dance together—a complex routine involving the manipulation of menus, check pads, wallets, checkbooks, credit cards, watches, pencils and paper napkins, which seemed to be hovering constantly on the edge of violence, but never actually getting anywhere.

Slartibartfast hurried in, and then appeared to pass the time of day quite idly with the maître d', while one of the customer robots, an autorory, slid slowly under the table, mentioning what he intended to do to some guy over some girl.

Slartibartfast took over the seat that had been thus vacated and passed a shrewd eye over the menu. The tempo of the routine around the table seemed somehow imperceptibly to quicken. Arguments broke out, people attempted to prove things on napkins. They waved fiercely at each other, and attempted to examine each other's pieces of chicken. The waiter's hand began to move on the check pad more quickly than a human hand could manage, and then more quickly than a human eye could follow. The pace accelerated. Soon, an extraordinary and insistent politeness overwhelmed the group, and seconds later it seemed that a moment of consensus was suddenly achieved. A new vibration thrilled through the ship.

Slartibartfast emerged from the glass room.

"Bistromathics," he said, "the most powerful computational force known to parascience. Come to the room of Informational Illusions."

He swept past and carried them, bewildered, in his wake.

Chapter 5

The Bistromathic Drive is a wonderful new method of crossing vast interstellar distances without all that dangerous mucking about with Improbability Factors.

Bistromathics itself is simply a revolutionary new way of understanding the behavior of numbers. Just as Einstein observed that space was not an absolute but depended on the observer's movement in space, and that time was not an absolute, but depended on the observer's movement in time, so it is now realized that numbers are not absolute, but depend on the observer's movement in restaurants.

The first nonabsolute number is the number of people for whom the table is reserved. This will vary during the course of the first three telephone calls to the restaurant, and then bear no apparent relation to the number of people who actually turn up, or to the number of people who subsequently join them after the show/match/party/gig, or to the number of people who leave when they see who else has turned up.

The second nonabsolute number is the given time of arrival, which is now known to be one of those most bizarre of mathematical concepts, a reciprriversexclusion, a number whose existence can only be defined as being anything other than itself. In other words, the given time of arrival is the one moment of time at which it is impossible that any member of the party will arrive. Recipriversexclusons now play a vital part in many branches of math, including statistics and accountancy and also form the basic equations used to engineer the Somebody Else's Problem field.

The third and most mysterious piece of nonabsoluteness of all lies in the relationship between the number of items on the check, the cost of each item, the number of people at the table and what they are each prepared to pay for. (The number of people who have actually brought any money is only a subphenomenon in this field.)

The baffling discrepancies that used to occur at this point remained uninvestigated for centuries simply because no one took them seriously. They were at the time put down to such things as politeness, rudeness, meanness, flashiness, tiredness, emotionality or the lateness of the hour, and completely forgotten about on the following morning. They were never tested under laboratory conditions, of course, because they never occurred in laboratories—not in reputable laboratories at least.

And so it was only with the advent of pocket computers that the startling truth became finally apparent, and it was this:

Numbers written on restaurant checks within the confines of restaurants do not follow the same mathematical laws as numbers written on any other pieces of paper in any other parts of the Universe.

This single statement took the scientific world by storm. It completely revolutionized it. So many mathematical conferences got held in such good restaurants

48

that many of the finest minds of a generation died of obesity and heart failure and the science of math was put back by years.

Slowly, however, the implications of the idea began to be understood. To begin with it had been too stark, too crazy, too much like what the man in the street would have said "Oh, yes, I could have told you that." Then some phrases like "Interactive Subjectivity Frameworks" were invented, and everybody was able to relax and get on with it.

The small groups of monks who had taken up hanging around the major research institutes singing strange chants to the effect that the Universe was only a figment of its own imagination were eventually given a street theater grant and went away.

Chapter 6

I n space travel, you see," said Slartibartfast, as he fiddled with some instruments in the room of Informational Illusions, "in space travel . . ."

He stopped and looked about him.

The room of Informational Illusions was a welcome relief after the visual monstrosities of the central computational area. There was nothing in it. No information, no illusions, just themselves, white walls and a few small instruments that looked as if they were meant to plug into something that Slartibartfast couldn't find.

"Yes?" urged Arthur. He had picked up Slartibartfast's sense of urgency but didn't know what to do with it.

"Yes what?" said the old man.

"You were saying?"

Slartibartfast looked at him sharply.

"The numbers," he said, "are awful." He resumed his search.

Arthur nodded wisely to himself. After a while he realized that this wasn't getting him anywhere and decided that he would say "What?" after all.

"In space travel," repeated Slartibartfast, "all the numbers are awful."

Arthur nodded again and looked around to Ford for help, but Ford was practicing being sullen and getting quite good at it.

"I was only," said Slartibartfast with a sigh, "trying to save you the trouble of asking me why all the ship's computations were being done on a waiter's check pad."

Arthur frowned.

"Why," he said, "were all the ship's computations being done on a wait—"

He stopped.

Slartibartfast said, "Because in space travel all the numbers are awful."

He could tell that he wasn't getting his point across.

"Listen," he said, "on a waiter's check pad numbers dance. You must have encountered the phenomenon."

"Well . . ."

"On a waiter's check pad," said Slartibartfast, "reality and unreality collide on such a fundamental level that each becomes the other and anything is possible, within certain parameters."

"What parameters?"

"It's impossible to say," said Slartibartfast. "That's one of them. Strange but true. At least, I think it's strange," he added, "and I am assured that it's true."

At that moment he located the slot in the wall for which he had been searching, and clicked the instrument he was holding into it.

"Do not be alarmed," he said, and then suddenly darted an alarmed look at it himself, and lunged back, "it's . . ."

They didn't hear what he said, because at that moment the ship winked out of existence around them and a star battleship the size of a small Midlands industrial city plunged out of the sundered night toward them, star lasers ablaze.

A nightmare storm of blistering light seared through the blackness and smacked a fair bit off the planet directly behind them.

They gaped, pop-eyed, and were unable to scream.

Chapter 7

nother world, another day, another dawn.
The early morning's thinnest sliver of
light appeared silently.

Several billion trillion tons of superhot exploding
hydrogen nuclei rose slowly above the horizon and
managed to look small, cold and slightly damp.

There is a moment in every dawn when light floats,
there is the possibility of magic. Creation holds its
breath.

The moment passed as it regularly did on Sqornshellous Zeta, without incident.

The mist clung to the surface of the marshes. The
swamp trees were gray with it, the tall reeds indistinct.
It hung motionless like held breath.

Nothing moved.

There was silence.

The sun struggled feebly with the mist, tried to im-
part a little warmth here, shed a little light there, but
clearly today was going to be just another long haul
across the sky.

Nothing moved.

Again, silence.

Nothing moved.

Silence.

Nothing moved.

Very often on Sqornshellous Zeta, whole days would go on like this, and this was indeed going to be one of them.

Fourteen hours later the sun sank hopelessly beneath the opposite horizon with a sense of totally wasted effort.

And a few hours later it reappeared, squared its shoulders and started on up the sky again.

This time, however, something was happening. A mattress had just met a robot.

"Hello, robot," said the mattress.

"Bleah," said the robot and continued what it was doing, which was walking round very slowly in a very tiny circle.

"Happy?" said the mattress.

The robot stopped and looked at the mattress. It looked at it quizzically. It was clearly a very stupid mattress. It looked back at him with wide eyes.

After what it had calculated to ten significant decimal places as being the precise length of pause most likely to convey a general contempt for all things mattressy, the robot continued to walk round in tight circles.

"We could have a conversation," said the mattress. "Would you like that?"

It was a large mattress, and probably one of quite high quality. Very few things actually get manufactured these days, because in an infinitely large Universe such as, for instance, the one in which we live, most things one could possibly imagine and a lot of things one would rather not, grow somewhere. (A forest was discovered recently in which most of the trees grew ratchet screwdrivers as fruit. The life cycle of ratchet screwdriver fruit is quite interesting. Once picked it needs a dark dusty drawer in which it can lie undisturbed for years. Then one night it suddenly hatches, discards its outer skin that crumbles into dust, and emerges as a totally unidentifiable little metal object with flanges at both ends and a sort of ridge and a sort of a hole for a screw. This, when found, will get thrown away. No one knows what it is supposed to gain from this. Nature, in her infinite wisdom, is presumably working on it.)

No one really knows what mattresses are meant to gain from their lives either. They are large, friendly, pocket-sprung creatures that live quiet private lives in the marshes of Sqornshellous Zeta. Many of them get caught, slaughtered, dried out, shipped out and slept on. None of them seems to mind this and all of them are called Zem.

"No," said Marvin.

"My name," said the mattress, "is Zem. We could discuss the weather a little."

Marvin paused again in his weary circular plod.

"The dew," he observed, "has clearly fallen with a particularly sickening thud this morning."

He resumed his walk, as if inspired by this conversational outburst to fresh heights of gloom and despondency. He plodded tenaciously. If he had had teeth he would have gritted them at this point. He hadn't. He didn't. The mere plod said it all.

The mattress flolloped around. This is a thing that only live mattresses in swamps are able to do, which is why the word is not in common usage. It flolloped in a sympathetic sort of way, moving a fair-size body of water as it did so. It blew a few bubbles up through the water engagingly. Its blue and white stripes glistened briefly in a sudden feeble ray of sun that had unexpectedly made it through the mist, causing the creature to bask momentarily.

Marvin plodded.

"You have something on your mind, I think," said the mattress, floopily.

"More than you can possibly imagine," dreared Marvin. "My capacity for mental activity of all kinds is as boundless as the infinite reaches of space itself. Except of course for my capacity for happiness."

Stomp, stomp, he went.

"My capacity for happiness," he added, "you could fit into a matchbox without taking out the matches first."

The mattress globbered. This is the noise made by a live, swamp-dwelling mattress that is deeply moved by a story of personal tragedy. The word can also, according to the *Ultra-Complete Maximegalon Dictionary of Every Language Ever*, mean the noise made by the Lord High Sanvalvwag of Hollop on discovering that he has forgotten his wife's birthday for the second year running. Since there was only ever one Lord High Sanvalvwag of Hollop and he never married, the word is only used in a negative or speculative sense, and there is an ever-increasing body of opinion that holds that the *Ultra-Complete Maximegalon Dictionary* is not worth the fleet of trucks it takes to cart its microstored edition around in. Strangely enough, the dictionary omits the word "floopily," which simply means "in the manner of something which is floopy."

The mattress globbered again.

"I sense a deep dejectedness in your diodes," it vollued (for the meaning of the word "vollue," buy a copy of *Sqornshellous Swamptalk* at any bookstore

56

selling remaindered books, or alternatively buy the *Ultra-Complete Maximegalon Dictionary*, as the university will be very glad to get it off their hands and regain some valuable parking lots), "and it saddens me. You should be more mattresslike. We live quiet retired lives in the swamp, where we are content to flollop and vollue and regard the wetness in a fairly floopy manner. Some of us are killed, but all of us are called Zem, so we never know which and globbering is thus kept to a minimum. Why are you walking in circles?"

"Because my leg is stuck," said Marvin simply.

"It seems to me," said the mattress, eying it compassionately, "that it is a pretty poor sort of leg."

"You are right," said Marvin, "it is."

"Voon," said the mattress.

"I expect so," said Marvin, "and I also expect that you find the idea of a robot with an artificial leg pretty amusing. You should tell your friends, Zem and Zem, when you see them later; they'll laugh, if I know them, which I don't of course, except insofar as I know all organic life-forms, which is much better than I would wish to. Ha, but my life is but a box of wormgears."

He stomped around again in his tiny circle, around his thin steel peg-leg that revolved in the mud but seemed otherwise stuck.

"But why do you just keep walking round and round?" asked the mattress.

"Just to make the point," said Marvin, and continued, round and round.

"Consider it made, my dear friend," flurbled the mattress, "consider it made."

"Just another million years," said Marvin, "just another quick million. Then I might try it backward. Just for the variety, you understand."

The mattress could feel deep in his innermost spring pockets that the robot dearly wished to be asked how long he had been trudging in this futile and fruitless manner, and with another quiet flurble he did so.

"Oh, just over the one point five million mark, just over," said Marvin airily; "ask me if I ever get bored, go on, ask me."

The mattress did.

Marvin ignored the question, he merely trudged with added emphasis.

"I gave a speech once," he said suddenly and apparently unconnectedly. "You may not instantly see why I bring the subject up, but that is because my mind works so phenomenally fast, and I am at a rough estimate thirty billion times more intelligent than you. Let me give you an example. Think of a number, any number."

"Er, five," said the mattress.

"Wrong," said Marvin. "You see?"

The mattress was much impressed by this and realized that it was in the presence of a not unremarkable mind. It willomied along its entire length sending excited little ripples through its shallow algae-covered pool.

It gupped.

"Tell me," it urged, "of the speech you once made, I long to hear it."

"It was received very badly," said Marvin, "for a variety of reasons. I delivered it," he added, pausing to make an awkward humping sort of gesture with his not-exactly-good arm, but his arm that was better than the other one that was dishearteningly welded to his left side, "over there, about a mile distant."

He was pointing as well as he could manage, and he obviously wanted to make it totally clear that this was as well as he could manage, through the mist, over the reeds, to a part of the marsh that looked exactly the same as every other part of the marsh.

"There," he repeated. "I was somewhat of a celebrity at the time."

Excitement gripped the mattress. It had never heard of speeches being delivered on Sqornshellous Zeta, and certainly not by celebrities. Water spattered off it as a thrill glurried across its back.

It did something that mattresses very rarely bother to do. Summoning every bit of its strength, it reared its oblong body, heaved it up into the air and held it quivering there for a few seconds until it peered through the mist over the reeds at the part of the marsh that Marvin had indicated, observing, without disappointment, that it was exactly the same as every other part of the marsh. The effort was too much, and it flodged back into its pool, deluging Marvin with smelly mud, moss and weeds.

"I was a celebrity," droned the robot sadly, "for a short while on account of my miraculous and bitterly resented escape from a fate almost as good as death in the heart of a blazing sun. You can guess from my condition," he added, "how narrow my escape was. I was rescued by a scrap-metal merchant, imagine that. Here I am, brain the size of . . . never mind."

He trudged savagely for a few seconds.

"He it was who fixed me up with this leg. Hateful, isn't it? He sold me to a Mind Zoo. I was the star exhibit. I had to sit on a box and tell my story while people told me to cheer up and think positive. 'Give us a grin, little robot,' they would shout at me, 'give us a little chuckle.' I would explain to them that to get my face to grin would take a good couple of hours in a workshop with a wrench, and that went down very well."

"The speech," urged the mattress, "I long to hear of the speech you gave in the marshes."

"There was a bridge built across the marshes. A cyberstructured hyperbridge, hundreds of miles in length, to carry ionbuggies and freighters over the swamp."

"A bridge?" quirruled the mattress, "here, in the swamp?"

"A bridge," confirmed Marvin, "here in the swamp. It was going to revitalize the economy of the Sqornshellous System. They spent the entire economy of the Sqornshellous System building it. They asked me to open it. Poor fools."

It began to rain a little, a fine spray slid through the mist.

"I stood on the platform. For hundreds of miles in front of me, and hundreds of miles behind me the bridge stretched."

"Did it glitter?" enthused the mattress.

"It glittered."

"Did it span the miles majestically?"

"It spanned the miles majestically."

"Did it stretch like a silver thread, far out into the invisible mist?"

"Yes," said Marvin, "do you want to hear this story?"

"I want to hear your speech," said the mattress.

"This is what I said. I said, 'I would like to say that

it is a very great pleasure, honor and privilege for me to open this bridge, but I can't because my lying circuits are all out of commission. I hate and despise you all. I now declare this hapless cyberstructure open to the unthinking abuse of all who wantonly cross her.' And I plugged myself into the opening circuits."

Marvin paused, remembering the moment.

The mattress flurred and glurried. It flolloped, gupped and willomied, doing this last in a particularly floopy way.

"Voon," it wurfed at last, "and was it a magnificent occasion?"

"Reasonably magnificent. The entire thousand-mile-long bridge spontaneously folded up its glittering spans and sank weeping into the mire, taking everybody with it."

There was a sad and terrible pause at this point in the conversation during which a hundred thousand people seemed unexpectedly to say "whop" and a team of white robots descended from the sky like dandelion seeds drifting on the wind in tight military formation. For a sudden violent moment they were all there, in the swamp, wrenching Marvin's false leg off, and then they were gone again in their ship that said "foop."

"You see the sort of thing I have to contend with?" said Marvin to the gobbering mattress.

And suddenly, a moment later, the robots were back again for another violent incident, and this time when they left, the mattress was alone in the swamp. He flolloped around in astonishment and alarm. He almost lurgled in fear. He reared himself to see over the reeds, but there was nothing to see, no robot, no glittering bridge, no ship, just more reeds. He listened, but there was no sound on the wind beyond the now familiar sound of half-crazed etymologists calling to each other across the sullen mire.

Chapter 8

The body of Arthur Dent spun.

The Universe shattered into a million glittering fragments around it, and each particular shard spun silently through the void, reflecting on its silver surface some single searing holocaust of fire and destruction.

And then the blackness behind the Universe exploded, and each particular piece of blackness was the furious smoke of hell.

And the nothingness behind the blackness behind the Universe erupted, and behind the nothingness behind the blackness behind the shattered Universe was at last the dark figure of an immense man speaking immense words.

"These, then," said the figure, speaking from an immensely comfortable chair, "were the Krikkit Wars, the greatest devastation ever visited upon our Galaxy. What you have experienced . . ."

Slartibartfast floated past, waving.

"It's just a documentary," he called out, "this is not a good bit. Terribly sorry, trying to find the rewind control . . ."

". . . is what billions upon billions of innocent . . ."

"Do not," called out Slartibartfast, floating past

again, and fiddling furiously with the thing that he had stuck into the wall of the room of Informational Illusions and that was in fact still stuck there, "agree to buy anything at this point."

". . . people, creatures, your fellow beings . . ."

Music swelled—again, it was immense music, immense chords. And behind the man, slowly, three tall pillars began slowly to emerge out of the immensely swirling mist.

". . . experienced, lived through or—more often—failed to live through. Think of that, my friends. And let us not forget—and in just a moment I shall be able to suggest a way that will help us always to remember—that before the Krikkit Wars, the Galaxy was that rare and wonderful thing, a happy Galaxy!"

The music was going bananas with immensity at this point.

"A happy Galaxy, my friends, as represented by the symbol of the Wikkit Gate!"

The three pillars stood out clearly now, three pillars topped with two crosspieces in a way that looked stupefyingly familiar to Arthur's addled brain.

"The three pillars," thundered the man, "the Steel Pillar, which represents the Strength and Power of the Galaxy!"

Searchlights seared out and danced crazy dances up and down the pillar on the left that was made of steel or something very like it. The music thumped and bellowed.

"The Plastic Pillar," announced the man, "representing the forces of Science and Reason in the Galaxy!"

Other searchlights played exotically up and down

the right-hand, transparent pillar creating dazzling patterns within it and a sudden inexplicable craving for ice cream in the stomach of Arthur Dent.

"And," the thunderous voice continued, "the Wooden Pillar, representing . . ." and here his voice became just very slightly hoarse with wonderful sentiments, "the forces of Nature and Spirituality."

The lights picked out the central pillar. The music moved bravely up into the realms of complete unspeakability.

"Between them supporting," the voice rolled on, approaching its climax, "the Golden Bail of Prosperity and the Silver Bail of Peace!"

The whole structure was now flooded with dazzling lights, and the music had now, fortunately, gone far beyond the limits of the discernible. At the top of the three pillars the two brilliantly gleaming bails sat and dazzled. There seemed to be girls sitting on top of them, or maybe they were meant to be angels. Angels usually are represented as wearing more than that though.

Suddenly there was a dramatic hush in what was presumably meant to be the cosmos, and a darkening of the lights.

"There is not a world," thrilled the man's expert voice, "not a civilized world in the Galaxy where this symbol is not revered even today. Even in primitive worlds it persists in racial memories. This it was that the forces of Krikkit destroyed, and this it is that now locks their world away till the end of eternity!"

And with a flourish, the man produced in his hands a model of the Wikkit Gate. Scale was terribly hard to judge in this whole extraordinary spectacle, but the model looked as if it must have been about three feet high.

"Not the original Key, of course. That, as everyone knows, was destroyed, blasted into the ever whirling eddies in the space-time continuum and lost forever. This is a remarkable replica, hand-tooled by skilled craftsmen, lovingly assembled using ancient craft secrets into a memento you will be proud to own, in memory of those who fell, and in tribute to the Galaxy—our Galaxy—which they died to defend. . . ."

Slartibartfast floated past again at this moment.

"Found it," he said, "we can lose all this rubbish. Just don't nod, that's all."

"Now, let us bow our heads in payment," intoned the voice, and then said it again, much faster and backward.

Lights came and went, the pillars disappeared, the man gabbled himself backward into nothing, the Universe snappily reassembled itself around them.

"You get the gist?" said Slartibartfast.

"I'm astonished," said Arthur, "and bewildered."

"I was asleep," said Ford, who floated into view at this point. "Did I miss anything?"

They found themselves once again teetering rather rapidly on the edge of an agonizingly high cliff. The wind whipped out from their faces and across a bay on which the remains of one of the greatest and most powerful space battle fleets ever assembled in the Galaxy were briskly burning themselves back into existence. The sky was a sullen pink, darkening, via a rather curious color, to blue and upward to black. Smoke billowed down out of it at an incredible lick.

Events were now passing back by them almost too quickly to be distinguished, and when, a short while later, a huge star battleship rushed away from them as if they'd said "Boo," they only just recognized it as the point at which they had come in.

But now things were too rapid, a videotactile blur that brushed and jiggled them through centuries of Galactic history, turning, twisting, flickering. The sound was a mere thin trill.

Periodically throughout the thickening jumble of events they sensed appalling catastrophies, deep horrors, cataclysmic shocks, and these were always associated with certain recurring images, the only images which ever stood out clearly from the avalanche of tumbling history: a Wikkit Gate, a small, hard red ball, and hard white robots, and also something less distinct, something dark and cloudy.

But there was also another sensation that rose clearly out of the trilling passage of time.

Just as a slow series of clicks when speeded up will lose the definition of each individual click and gradually take on the quality of a sustained and rising tone, so a series of individual impressions here took on the quality of a sustained emotion—and yet not an emotion. If it was an emotion, it was a totally emotionless one. It was hatred, implacable hatred. It was cold, not like ice is cold, but like a wall is cold. It was impersonal, not like a randomly flung fist in a crowd is impersonal, but like a computer-issued parking summons is impersonal. And it was deadly, again, not like a bullet or a knife is deadly, but like a brick wall across an expressway is deadly.

And just as a rising tone will change in character and take on harmonics as it rises, so again this emotionless emotion seemed to rise to an unbearable if unheard scream and suddenly seemed to be a scream of guilt and failure.

And suddenly it stopped.

They were left standing on a quiet hilltop on a tranquil evening.

The sun was setting.

All around them softly undulating green countryside rolled off gently into the distance. Birds sang about what they thought of it all, and the general opinion seemed to be good. A little way off could be heard the sound of children playing, and a little farther away than the apparent source of that sound could be seen in the dimming evening light the outlines of a small town.

The town appeared to consist mostly of fairly low buildings made of white stone. The skyline was of gentle pleasing curves.

The sun had nearly set.

As if out of nowhere, music began. Slartibartfast tugged at a switch and it stopped.

A voice said, "This ..." Slartibartfast tugged at a switch and it stopped.

"I will tell you about it," he said quietly.

The place was peaceful. Arthur felt happy. Even Ford seemed cheerful. They walked a short way in the direction of the town, and the Informational Illusion of the grass was pleasant and springy under their feet, and the Informational Illusion of the flowers smelled sweet and fragrant. Only Slartibartfast seemed apprehensive and out of sorts.

He stopped and looked up.

It suddenly occurred to Arthur that coming as this did at the end, so to speak, or rather the beginning, of all the horror they had just blurrily experienced, something nasty must be about to happen. He was distressed to think that something nasty could happen to somewhere as idyllic as this. He too glanced up. There was nothing in the sky.

"They're not about to attack here, are they?" he said. He realized that this was merely a recording he was walking through, but he still felt alarmed.

"Nothing is about to attack here," said Slartibartfast in a voice that unexpectedly trembled with emotion, "this is where it all starts. This is the place itself. This is Krikkit."

He stared up into the sky.

The sky, from one horizon to another, from east to west, from north to south, was utterly and completely black.

Chapter 9

Stomp stomp.
Whirrr.
"Pleased to be of service."
"Shut up."
"Thank you."
Stomp stomp stomp stomp stomp.
Whirrr.
"Thank you for making a simple door very happy."
"Hope your diodes rot."
"Thank you. Have a nice day."
Stomp stomp stomp stomp.
Whirrr.
"It is my pleasure to open for you . . ."
"Zark off."
". . . and my satisfaction to close again with the knowledge of a job well done."
"I said zark off."
"Thank you for listening to this message."
Stomp stomp stomp stomp.
"Whop."

Zaphod stopped stomping. He had been stomping around the *Heart of Gold* for days, and so far no door had said "whop" to him. He was fairly certain that no door had said "whop" to him now. It was not the sort of thing doors said. Too concise. Furthermore, there were not enough doors. It sounded as if a hundred thousand people had said "whop," which puzzled him because he was the only person on the ship.

It was dark. Most of the ship's nonessential systems were closed down. It was drifting idly in a remote area of the Galaxy, deep in the inky blackness of space. So which particular hundred thousand people would turn up at this point and say a totally unexpected "whop"?

He looked about him, up the corridor and down the corridor. It was all in deep shadow. There were just the very dim pinkish outlines to the doors that glowed in the dark and pulsed whenever they spoke though he had tried every way he could think of to stop them.

The lights were off so that his heads could avoid looking at each other because neither of them was currently a particularly engaging sight, nor had they been since he had made the error of looking into his soul.

It had indeed been an error.

It had been late one night—of course.

It had been a difficult day—of course.

There had been soulful music playing on the ship's sound system—of course.

And he had, of course, been slightly drunk.

In other words, all the usual conditions that bring on a bout of soul-searching had applied, but it had, nevertheless, clearly been an error.

Standing now, silent and alone in the dark corridor, he remembered the moment and shivered. His one head looked one way and his other the other and each decided that the other way was the way to go.

He listened but could hear nothing.

All there had been was the "whop."

71

It seemed an awfully long way to bring an awfully large number of people just to say one word.

He started nervously to edge his way in the direction of the bridge. There at least he would feel in control. He stopped again. The way he was feeling he didn't think he was an awfully good person to be in control.

The first shock of that moment, thinking back, had been discovering that he actually had a soul.

In fact he'd always more or less assumed that he had one as he had a full complement of everything else, and indeed two of some things, but suddenly actually to encounter the thing lurking there deep within him had given him a severe jolt.

And then to discover (this was the second shock) that it wasn't the totally wonderful object that he felt a man in his position had a natural right to expect had jolted him again.

Then he had thought about what his position actually was and the renewed shock had nearly made him spill his drink. He drained it quickly before anything serious happened to it. He then had another quick one to follow the first one down and check that it was all right.

"Freedom," he said aloud.

Trillian came onto the bridge at that point and said several enthusiastic things on the subject of freedom.

"I can't cope with it," he said darkly, and sent a third drink down to see why the second hadn't yet reported on the condition of the first. He looked uncertainly at both of her and preferred the one on the right.

He poured a drink down his other throat with the plan that it would head the previous one off at the pass, join forces with it, and together they would get the second to pull itself together. Then all three would go off in search of the first, give it a good talking to.

He felt uncertain as to whether the fourth drink had understood all that so he sent down a fifth to explain the plan more fully and a sixth for moral support.

"You're drinking too much," said Trillian.

His heads collided trying to sort out the four of her he could now see into a whole person. He gave up and looked at the navigation screen and was astonished to see a quite phenomenal number of stars.

"Excitement and adventure and really wild things," he muttered.

"Look," she said in sympathetic tone of voice, and sat down near him, "it's quite understandable that you're going to feel a little aimless for a bit."

He boggled at her. He had never seen anyone sit on their own lap before.

"Wow," he said. He had another drink.

"You've finished the mission you've been on for years."

"I haven't been on it. I've tried to avoid being on it."

"You've still finished it."

He grunted. There seemed to be a terrific party going on in his stomach.

"I think it finished me," he said. "Here I am, Zaphod Beeblebrox, I can go anywhere, do anything. I have the greatest ship in the known sky, a girl with whom things seem to be working out pretty well. . . ."

"Are they?"

"As far as I can tell. I'm not an expert in personal relationships. . . ."

Trillian raised her eyebrows.

"I am," he added, "one hell of a guy, I can do anything I want only I just don't have the faintest idea what."

He paused.

"One thing," he further added, "has suddenly ceased to lead to another," in contradiction of which he had another drink and slid gracelessly off his chair.

While he slept it off, Trillian did a little research in the ship's copy of *The Hitchhiker's Guide to the Galaxy*. It had some advice to offer on drunkenness.

"Go to it," it said, "and good luck."

It was cross-referenced to the entry concerning the size of the Universe and ways of coping with that.

Then she found the entry on Han Wavel, an exotic holiday planet, and one of the wonders of the Galaxy. Han Wavel is a world that consists largely of fabulous ultraluxury hotels and casinos, all of which have been formed by the natural erosion of wind and rain.

The chances of this happening are more or less one to infinity against. Little is known of how this came about because none of the geophysicists, probability statisticians, meteoranalysts or bizarrologists who are so keen to research it can afford to stay there.

"Terrific," thought Trillian to herself, and within a few hours, the great white running-shoe ship was slowly powering down out of the sky beneath a hot brilliant sun toward a brightly colored sandy spaceport. The ship was clearly causing a sensation on the ground, and Trillian was enjoying herself. She heard Zaphod moving around and whistling somewhere in the ship.

"How are you?" she said over the general intercom.

"Fine," he said brightly, "terribly well."

"Where are you?"

"In the bathroom."

"What are you doing?"

"Staying here."

After an hour or two it became clear that he meant it and the ship returned to the sky without having once opened its hatchway.

"Heigh-ho," said Eddie the Computer.

Trillian nodded patiently, tapped her fingers a couple of times and pushed the intercom switch.

"I think that enforced fun is probably not what you need at this point."

"Probably not," replied Zaphod from wherever he was.

"I think a bit of physical challenge would help draw you out of yourself."

"Whatever you think, I think," said Zaphod.

RECREATIONAL IMPOSSIBILITIES was a heading that caught Trillian's eye when, a short while later, she sat down to flip through the *Guide* again, and as the *Heart of Gold* rushed at improbable speeds in an indeterminate direction, she sipped a cup of something undrinkable from the Nutri-matic Drinks Dispenser and read about how to fly.

The Hitchhiker's Guide to the Galaxy has this to say on the subject of flying.

There is an art, it says, or, rather, a knack to flying.

The knack lies in learning how to throw yourself at the ground and miss.

Pick a nice day, it suggests, and try it.

The first part is easy.

All it requires is simply the ability to throw yourself forward with all your weight, and the willingness not to mind that it's going to hurt.

That is, it's going to hurt if you fail to miss the ground.

Most people fail to miss the ground, and if they are really trying properly, the likelihood is that they will fail to miss it fairly hard.

Clearly, it is this second part, the missing, which presents the difficulties.

One problem is that you have to miss the ground accidentally. It's no good deliberately intending to miss the ground because you won't. You have to have your attention suddenly distracted by something else when you're halfway there, so that you are no longer thinking about falling, or about the ground, or about how much it's going to hurt if you fail to miss it.

It is notoriously difficult to prize your attention away from these three things during the split second you have at your disposal. Hence most people's failure, and their eventual disillusionment with this exhilarating and spectacular sport.

If, however, you are lucky enough to have your attention momentarily distracted at the crucial moment by, say, a gorgeous pair of legs (tentacles, pseudopodia, according to phyllum and/or personal inclination) or a bomb going off in your vicinity, or by suddenly spotting an extremely rare species of beetle crawling along a nearby twig, then in your astonishment you will miss the ground completely and remain bobbing just a few inches above it in what might seem to be a slightly foolish manner.

This is a moment for superb and delicate concentration.

Bob and float, float and bob.

Ignore all considerations of your own weight and simply let yourself waft higher.

Do not listen to what anybody says to you at this

point because they are unlikely to say anything help-ful.

They are most likely to say something along the lines of "Good God, you can't possibly be flying!"

It is vitally important not to believe them or they will suddenly be right.

Waft higher and higher.

Try a few swoops, gentle ones at first, then drift above the treetops breathing regularly.

DO NOT WAVE AT ANYBODY.

When you have done this a few times you will find the moment of distraction rapidly becomes easier and easier to achieve.

You will then learn all sorts of things about how to control your flight, your speed, your maneuverability, and the trick usually lies in not thinking too hard about whatever you want to do, but just allowing it to happen as if it were going to anyway.

You will also learn about how to land properly, which is something you will almost certainly screw up, and screw up badly, on your first attempt.

There are private flying clubs you can join which help you achieve the all-important moment of distraction. They hire people with surprising bodies or opinions to leap out from behind bushes and exhibit and/or explain them at the critical moments. Few genuine hitchhikers will be able to afford to join these clubs, but some may be able to get temporary employment at them.

Trillian read this longingly, but reluctantly decided that Zaphod wasn't really in the right frame of mind for attempting to fly, or for walking through mountains or for trying to get the Brantisvogan Civil Service to acknowledge a change of address card, which were the other things listed under the heading of REC-REATIONAL IMPOSSIBILITIES.

Instead, she flew the ship to Allosimanius Syneca, a world of ice, snow, mind-hurtling beauty and stunning cold. The trek from the snow plains of Liska to the summit of the Ice Crystal Pyramids of Sastantua is long and grueling, even with jet skis and a team of Syneca Snowhounds, but the view from the top, a view which takes in the Stin Glacier Fields, the shimmering Prism Mountains and the far ethereal dancing icelights, is one which first freezes the mind and then slowly releases it to hitherto unexperienced horizons of beauty, and Trillian, for one, felt that she could do with a bit of having her mind slowly released to hitherto unexperienced horizons of beauty.

They went into a low orbit.

There lay the silverwhite beauty of Allosimanius Syneca beneath them.

Zaphod stayed in bed with one head stuck under a pillow and the other doing crosswords till late into the night.

Trillian nodded patiently again, counted to a sufficiently high number, and told herself that the important thing now was just to get Zaphod talking.

She prepared, by dint of deactivating all the robot kitchen synthomatics, the most fabulously delicious meal she could contrive—delicately oiled meats, scented fruits, fragrant cheeses, fine Aldebaran wines.

She carried it through to him and asked if he felt like talking things through.

"Zark off," said Zaphod.

Trillian nodded patiently to herself, counted to an even higher number, tossed the tray lightly aside, walked to the transport room and just teleported herself the hell out of his life.

She didn't even program any coordinates, she hadn't the faintest idea where she was going, she just went—a random row of dots flowing through the Universe.

"Anything," she said to herself as she left, "is better than this."

"Good job, too," muttered Zaphod to himself, turned over and failed to go to sleep.

The next day he restlessly paced the empty corridors of the ship, pretending not to look for her, though he knew she wasn't there. He ignored the computer's querulous demands to know just what the hell was going on around here by fitting a small electronic gag across a pair of its terminals.

After a while he began to turn down the lights. There was nothing to see. Nothing was about to happen.

Lying in bed one night—and night was now virtually continuous on the ship—he decided to pull himself together, to get things into some kind of perspective. He sat up sharply and started to pull clothes on. He decided that there must be someone in the Universe feeling more wretched, miserable and forsaken than himself, and he determined to set out and find him.

Halfway to the bridge it occurred to him that it might be Marvin and he returned to bed.

It was a few hours later than this as he stomped disconsolately about the darkened corridors swearing at cheerful doors, that he heard the "whop" said, and it made him very nervous.

He leaned tensely against the corridor wall and

frowned like a man trying to unbend a corkscrew by telekinesis. He laid his fingertips against the wall and felt an unusual vibration. And now he could quite clearly hear slight noises, and could hear where they were coming from—they were coming from the bridge.

Moving his hand along the wall he came across something he was glad to find. He moved on a little farther, quietly.

"Computer?" he hissed.

"Mmmm?" said the computer terminal nearest him, equally quietly.

"Is there someone on this ship?"

"Mmmm," said the computer.

"Who is it?"

"Mmmm mmm mmmmm," said the computer.

"What?"

"Mmmmm mmmm mm mmmmmmmm."

Zaphod buried one of his faces in two of his hands.

"Oh, Zarquon," he muttered to himself. Then he stared up the corridor toward the entrance to the bridge in the dim distance from which more and purposeful noises were coming, and in which the gagged terminals were situated.

"Computer," he hissed again.

"Mmmmm?"

"When I ungag you . . ."

"Mmmmm."

"Remind me to punch myself in the mouth."

"Mmmmm mmm?"

"Either one. Now just tell me this. One for yes, two for no. Is it dangerous?"

"Mmmm."

"It is?"

80

"Mmmm."

"You didn't just go 'mmmm' twice?"

"Mmmm mmm."

"Hmmmm."

He inched his way up the corridor as if he would rather be yarding his way down it, which was true.

He was within two yards of the door to the bridge when he suddenly realized to his horror that it was going to be nice to him, and he stopped dead. He hadn't been able to turn off the door's courtesy voice circuits.

This doorway to the bridge was concealed from view within it because of the excitingly chunky way in which the bridge had been designed to curve round, and he had been hoping to enter unobserved.

He leaned despondently back against the wall again and said some words that his other head was quite shocked to hear.

He peered at the dim pink outline of the door, and discovered that in the darkness of the corridor he could just about make out the Sensor Field that extended out into the corridor and told the door when there was someone there for whom it must open and to whom it must make a cheery and pleasant remark.

He pressed himself hard back against the wall and edged himself toward the door, flattening his chest as much as he possibly could to avoid brushing against the very, very dim perimeter of the field. He held his breath, and congratulated himself on having lain in bed sulking for the last few days rather than trying to work out his feelings on chest expanders in the ship's gym.

He then realized he was going to have to speak at this point.

He took a series of very shallow breaths, and then

said as quickly and as quietly as he could, "Door, if you can hear me, say so very, very quietly."

Very, very quietly, the door murmured, "I can hear you."

"Good. Now, in a moment, I'm going to ask you to open. When you open I do not want you to say that you enjoyed it, okay?"

"Okay."

"And I don't want you to say to me that I have made a simple door very happy, or that it is your pleasure to open for me and your satisfaction to close again with the knowledge of a job well done, okay?"

"Okay."

"And I do not want you to ask me to have a nice day, understand?"

"I understand."

"Okay," said Zaphod, tensing himself, "open now."

The door slid open quietly. Zaphod slipped quietly through. The door closed quietly behind him.

"Is that the way you like it, Mr. Beeblebrox?" said the door out loud.

"I want you to imagine," said Zaphod to the group of white robots who swung round to stare at him at that point, "that I have an extremely powerful Kill-O-Zap blaster pistol in my hand."

There was an immensely cold and savage silence. The robots regarded him with hideously dead eyes. They stood very still. There was something intensely macabre about their appearance, especially to Zaphod, who had never seen one before or even known anything about them. The Krikkit Wars belonged to the ancient past of the Galaxy, and Zaphod had spent most of his early history lessons plotting how he was going to have sex with the girl in the cybercubicle next to him, and since his teaching computer had been an integral part of this plot it had eventually had all its history circuits wiped and replaced with an entirely different set of ideas that had then resulted in its being scrapped and sent to a home for Degenerate Cybermats, whither it was followed by the girl who had inadvertently fallen deeply in love with the unfortunate machine, with the result that (a) Zaphod never got near her and (b) he missed out on a period of ancient history that would have been of inestimable value to him at this moment.

He stared at them in shock.

It was impossible to explain why, but their smooth and sleek white bodies seemed to be the utter embodiment of clean, clinical evil. From their hideously dead eyes to their powerful lifeless feet, they were clearly the calculated product of a mind that wanted simply to kill. Zaphod gulped in cold fear.

They had been dismantling part of the rear wall, and had forced a passage through some of the vital innards of the ship. Through the tangled wreckage Zaphod could see, with a further and worse sense of shock, that they were tunneling toward the very heart of the ship, the heart of the Improbability Drive that had been so mysteriously created out of thin air, the *Heart of Gold* itself.

The robot closest to him was regarding him in such a way as to suggest that it was measuring each minute particle of his body, mind and capability. And when it spoke, what it said seemed to bear this impression out. Before going on to what it actually said, it is worth recording at this point that Zaphod was the first living organic being to hear one of these creatures speak for something over ten billion years. If he had paid more attention to his ancient history lessons and less to his organic being, he might have been more impressed by this honor.

The robot's voice was like its body, cold, sleek and lifeless. It had almost a cultured rasp to it. It sounded as ancient as it was.

It said, "You do have a Kill-O-Zap blaster pistol in your hand."

Zaphod didn't know what it meant for a moment, but then he glanced down at his own hand and was relieved to see that what he had found clipped to a wall bracket was indeed what he had thought it was.

"Yeah," he said in a kind of relieved sneer, which is quite tricky, "well, I wouldn't want to overtax your imagination, robot."

For a while nobody said anything, and Zaphod realized that the robots were obviously not here to make conversation, and that it was up to him.

"I can't help noticing that you have parked your ship," he said with a nod of one of his heads in the appropriate direction, "through mine."

There was no denying this. Without regard for any kind of proper dimensional behavior they had simply materialized their ship precisely where they wanted it to be, which meant that it was simply locked through the *Heart of Gold* as if they were nothing more than two combs.

Again, they made no response to this, and Zaphod wondered if the conversation would gather any momentum if he phrased his part of it in the form of questions.

"Haven't you?" he added.

"Yes," replied the robot.

"Er, okay," said Zaphod, "so what are you cats doing here?"

Silence.

"Robots," said Zaphod, "what are you robots doing here?"

"We have come," rasped the robot, "for the Golden Bail."

Zaphod nodded. He waggled his gun to invite further elaboration. The robot seemed to understand this.

"The Golden Bail is part of the Key we seek," continued the robot, "to release our Masters from Krikkit."

Zaphod nodded again. He waggled his gun again.

"The Key," continued the robot simply, "was disintegrated in time and space. The Golden Bail is embedded in the device which drives your ship. It will be reconstituted in the Key. Our Masters shall be released. The Universal Readjustment will continue."

Zaphod nodded again.

"What are you talking about?" he said.

A slightly pained expression seemed to cross the robot's totally expressionless face. He seemed to be finding the conversation depressing.

"Obliteration," it said. "We seek the Key," it repeated. "We already have the Wooden Pillar, the Steel Pillar and the Plastic Pillar. In a moment we will have the Golden Bail. . . ."

"No, you won't."

"We will," stated the robot simply.

"No, you won't. It makes my ship work."

"In a moment," repeated the robot patiently, "we will have the Golden Bail. . . ."

"You will not," said Zaphod.

"And then we must go," said the robot, in all seriousness, "to a party."

"Oh," said Zaphod, startled, "can I come?"

"No," said the robot, "we are going to shoot you."

"Oh, yeah?" said Zaphod, waggling his gun.

"Yes," said the robot, and they shot him.

Zaphod was so surprised that they had to shoot him again before he fell down.

Chapter 10

Shhh," said Slartibartfast, "listen and watch."

Night had now fallen on ancient Krikkit. The sky was dark and empty. The only light was coming from the nearby town, from which pleasant convivial sounds were drifting quietly on the breeze. They stood beneath a tree from which heady fragrances wafted around them. Arthur squatted and felt the Informational Illusion of the soil and the grass. He ran it through his fingers. The soil seemed heavy and rich, the grass strong. It was hard to avoid the impression that this was a thoroughly delightful place in all respects.

The sky was, however, extremely blank and seemed to Arthur to cast a certain chill over the otherwise idyllic, if currently invisible, landscape. Still, he supposed, it's a question of what you're used to.

He felt a tap on his shoulder and looked up. Slartibartfast was quietly directing his attention to something down the other side of the hill. He looked and could just see some faint lights dancing and waving, and moving slowly in their direction.

As they came nearer sounds became audible, too, and soon the dim lights and noises resolved themselves into a small group of people who were walking home across the hill toward the town.

They walked quite near the watchers beneath the tree, swinging lanterns that made soft and crazy lights dance among the trees and grass, chattering contentedly, and actually singing a song about how terribly nice everything was, how happy they were, how much they enjoyed working on the farm, and how pleasant it was to be going home to see their wives and children, with a lilting chorus to the effect that the flowers were smelling particularly nice at this time of year and that it was a pity the dog had died seeing as it liked them so much. Arthur could almost imagine Paul McCartney sitting with his feet up by the fire one evening, humming it to Linda and wondering what to buy with the proceeds, and thinking, probably, Essex.

"The Masters of Krikkit," breathed Slartibartfast in sepulchral tones.

Coming, as it did, so hard upon the heels of his own thoughts about Essex this remark caused Arthur a moment's confusion. Then the logic of the situation imposed itself on his scattered mind, and he discovered that he still didn't understand what the old man meant.

"What?" he said.

"The Masters of Krikkit," said Slartibartfast again, and if his breathing had been sepulchral before, this time he sounded like someone in Hades with bronchitis.

Arthur peered at the group and tried to make sense of what little information he had at his disposal at this point.

The people in the group were clearly alien, if only because they seemed a little tall, thin, angular and al-

most as pale as to be white, but otherwise seemed re-
markably pleasant, a little whimsical perhaps; one
wouldn't necessarily want to spend a long bus journey
with them, but the point was that if they deviated in
any way from being good straightforward people it
was in being perhaps too nice rather than not nice
enough. So why all this rasping lungwork from
Slartibartfast, which would seem more appropriate to
a radio commercial for one of those nasty films about
chain-saw operators taking their work home with
them?

Then, this Krikkit angle was a tough one, too. He
hadn't quite fathomed the connection between what he
knew as cricket, and what . . .

Slartibartfast interrupted his train of thought at this
point as if sensing what was going through his mind.

"The game you know as cricket," he said, and his
voice still seemed to be wandering, lost in subterra-
nean passages, "is just one of those curious freaks of
racial memory that can keep images alive in the mind
eons after their true significance has been lost in the
mists of time. Of all the races in the Galaxy, only the
English could possibly revive the memory of the most
horrific wars ever to sunder the Universe and trans-
form it into what I'm afraid is generally regarded as
an incomprehensibly dull and pointless game.

"Rather fond of it myself," he added, "but in most
people's eyes you have been inadvertently guilty of
the most grotesquely bad taste. Particularly the bit
about the little red ball hitting the wicket, that's very
nasty."

"Um," said Arthur with a reflective frown to indicate that his cognitive synapses were coping with this
as best they could, "um."

"And these," said Slartibartfast, slipping back into crypt guttural and indicating the group of Krikkit men who had now walked past them, "are the ones who started it all, and it will start tonight. Come, we will follow, and see why."

They slipped out from underneath the tree, and followed the cheery party along the dark hill path. Their natural instinct was to tread quietly and stealthily in pursuit of their quarry, though, as they were simply walking through a recorded Informational Illusion, they could as easily have been carrying euphoniums and wearing war paint for all the notice their quarry would have taken of them.

Arthur saw that a couple of members of the party were now singing a different song. It came lilting back to them through the soft night air, and was a sweet romantic ballad that would have netted McCartney Kent and Sussex and enabled him to put in a fair offer for Hampshire.

"You must surely know," said Slartibartfast to Ford, "what it is that is about to happen?"

"Me?" said Ford, "no."

"Did you not learn Ancient Galactic history when you were a child?"

"I was in the cybercubicle behind Zaphod," said Ford; "it was very distracting. Which isn't to say that I didn't learn some pretty stunning things."

At this point Arthur noticed a curious feature to the song that the party was singing. The middle eight bridge, which would have had McCartney firmly consolidated in Winchester and gazing intently over the Test Valley to the rich pickings of the New Forest beyond, had some curious lyrics. The songwriter was referring to meeting with a girl not "under the moon" or "beneath the stars" but "above the grass," which struck Arthur as being a little prosaic. Then he looked up again at the bewilderingly blank sky, and had the distinct feeling that there was an important point here, if only he could grasp what it was. It gave him a feeling of being alone in the Universe, and he said so.

"No," said Slartibartfast, with a slight quickening of his step, "the people of Krikkit have never thought to themselves, 'We are alone in the Universe.' They are surrounded by a huge Dust Cloud, you see, their single sun with its single world, and they are right out on the utmost eastern edge of the Galaxy. Because of the Dust Cloud there has never been anything to see in the sky. At night it is totally blank. During the day there is the sun, but you can't look directly at that so they don't. They are hardly aware of the sky. It's as if they had a blind spot that extended 180 degrees from horizon to horizon.

"You see, the reason why they have never thought, 'We are alone in the Universe' is that until tonight they didn't know about the Universe. Until tonight."

He moved on, leaving the words ringing in the air behind him.

"Imagine," he said, "never even thinking, 'We are alone,' simply because it has never occurred to you to think that there's any other way to be."

He moved on again.

"I'm afraid this is going to be a little unnerving," he added.

As he spoke, they became aware of a very thin roaring scream high up in the sightless sky above them. They glanced upward in alarm, but for a moment or two could see nothing.

Then Arthur noticed that the people in the party in

front of them had heard the noise, but that none of them seemed to know what to do with it. They were glancing around themselves in consternation, left, right, forward, backward, even at the ground. It never occurred to them to look upward.

The profoundness of the shock and horror they emanated a few moments later when the burning wreckage of a spaceship came hurtling and screaming out of the sky and crashed about half a mile from where they were standing was something that you had to be there to experience.

Some speak of the *Heart of Gold* in hushed tones, some of the starship *Bistromath*.

Many speak of the legendary and gigantic starship *Titanic*, a majestic and luxurious cruise liner launched from the great shipbuilding asteroid complexes of Artrifactovol some hundreds of years ago now, and with good reason.

It was sensationally beautiful, staggeringly huge and more pleasantly equipped than any ship in what now remains of history (see page 113 [on the Campaign for Real Time]) but it had the misfortune to be built in the very earliest days of Improbability Physics, long before this difficult and cussed branch of knowledge was fully, or at all, understood.

The designers and engineers decided, in their innocence, to build a prototype Improbability Field into it, which was meant, supposedly, to ensure that it was Infinitely Improbable that anything would ever go wrong with any part of the ship.

They did not realize that because of the quasi-reciprocal and circular nature of all Improbability calculations, anything that was Infinitely Improbable was actually very likely to happen almost immediately.

The starship *Titanic* was a monstrously pretty sight as it lay beached like a silver Arcturan Megavoidwhale among the laserlit tracery of its construction gantries, a brilliant cloud of pins and needles of light against the deep interstellar blackness; but when launched, it did not even manage to complete its very first radio message—an SOS—before undergoing a sudden and gratuitous total existence failure.

However, the same event that saw the disastrous failure of one science in its infancy also witnessed the apotheosis of another. It was conclusively proved that more people watched the Tri-D television coverage of the launch than actually existed at the time, and this has now been recognized as the greatest achievement ever in the science of audience research.

Another spectacular media event of that time was the supernova that the star Ysllodins underwent a few hours later. Ysllodins is the star around which most of the Galaxy's major insurance underwriters live, or rather lived.

But while these spaceships, and other great ones that come to mind, such as the Galactic Fleet Battleships—the GSS *Daring*, the GSS *Audacity* and the GSS *Suicidal Insanity*—are all spoken of with awe, pride, enthusiasm, affection, admiration, regret, jealousy, resentment, in fact most of the better known emotions, the one that regularly commands the most actual astonishment is *Krikkit One*, the first spaceship ever built by the people of Krikkit.

This is not because it was a wonderful ship. It wasn't.

It was a crazy piece of near-junk. It looked as if it

had been knocked up in somebody's backyard, and this was in fact precisely where it had been knocked up. The astonishing thing about the ship was not that it was done well (it wasn't) but that it was done at all. The period of time that had elapsed between the moment that the people of Krikkit had discovered that there was such a thing as space and the launching of this, their first spaceship, was almost exactly a year.

Ford Prefect was extremely grateful, as he strapped himself in, that this was just another Informational Illusion, and that he was therefore completely safe. In real life it wasn't a ship he would have set foot in for all the rice wine in China. "Extremely rickety" was one phrase that sprang to mind and "Please may I get out?" was another.

"This is going to fly?" said Arthur, giving gaunt looks at the lashed-together pipework and wiring that festooned the cramped interior of the ship.

Slartibartfast assured him that it would, that they were perfectly safe and that it was all going to be extremely instructive and not a little harrowing.

Ford and Arthur decided just to relax and be harrowed.

"Why not," said Ford, "go mad?"

In front of them and, of course, totally unaware of their presence for the very good reason that they weren't actually there, were the three pilots. They also had constructed the ship. They had been on the hill path that night singing wholesome, heartwarming songs. Their brains had been very slightly turned by the nearby crash of the alien spaceship. They had spent weeks stripping every tiniest last secret out of the wreckage of that burnt-up spaceship, all the while singing lilting spaceship-stripping ditties. They had then built their own ship and this was it. This was their ship, and they were currently singing a little song about that, too, expressing the twin joys of achievement and ownership. The chorus was a little poignant, and told of their sorrow because their work had kept them such long hours in the garage, away from the company of their wives and children, who had missed them terribly but had kept them cheerful by bringing them continual stories of how nicely the puppy was growing up.

Pow, they took off.

They roared into the sky like a ship that knew precisely what it was doing.

"No way," said Ford a while later after they had recovered from the shock of acceleration, and were climbing up out of the planet's atmosphere, "no way," he repeated, "does anyone design and build a ship like this in a year, no matter how motivated. I don't believe it. Prove it to me and I still won't believe it." He shook his head thoughtfully and gazed out of a tiny port at the nothingness outside it.

The trip passed uneventfully for a while, and Slartibartfast fastwound them through it.

Very quickly, therefore, they arrived at the inner perimeter of the hollow, spherical Dust Cloud that surrounded their sun and home planet, occupying, as it were, the next orbit out.

It was more as if there were a gradual change in the texture and consistency of space. The darkness seemed now to thrum and ripple past them. It was very cold darkness, a very blank and heavy darkness, it was the darkness of the night sky of Krikkit.

The coldness and heaviness and blankness of it took a slow grip on Arthur's heart, and he felt acutely aware of the feelings of the Krikkit pilots that hung in the air like a thick static charge. They were now on the very boundary of the historical consciousness of their race. This was the very limit beyond which none of them had ever speculated, or even known that there was any speculation to be done.

The darkness of the cloud buffeted at the ship. Inside was the silence of history. Their historic mission was to find out if there was anything or anywhere on the other side of the sky, from which the wrecked spaceship could have come, another world maybe, strange and incomprehensible though this thought was to the enclosed minds of those who had lived beneath the sky of Krikkit.

History was gathering itself to deliver another blow.

Still the darkness thrummed at them, the blank enclosing darkness. It seemed closer and closer, thicker and thicker, heavier and heavier. And suddenly it was gone.

They flew out of the cloud.

They saw the staggering jewels of the night in their infinite dust and their minds sang with fear.

For a while they flew on, motionless against the starry sweep of the Galaxy, itself motionless against the infinite sweep of the Universe. And then they turned round.

"It'll have to go," the men of Krikkit said as they headed back for home.

On the way back they sang a number of tuneful and reflective songs on the subjects of peace, justice, morality, culture, sport, family life and the obliteration of all other life-forms.

Chapter 11

S o you see," said Slartibartfast, slowly stirring his artificially constructed coffee, and thereby also stirring the whirlpool interfaces between real and unreal numbers, between the interactive perceptions of mind and universe, and thus generating the restructured matrices of implicitly enfolded subjectivity that allowed his ship to reshape the very concept of time and space, "how it is."

"Yes," said Arthur.

"Yes," said Ford.

"What do I do," said Arthur, "with this piece of chicken?"

Slartibartfast glanced at him, gravely.

"Toy with it," he said, "toy with it."

He demonstrated with his own piece.

Arthur did so, and felt the slight tingle of a mathematical function thrilling through the chicken leg as it moved four-dimensionally through what Slartibartfast had assured him was five-dimensional space.

"Overnight," said Slartibartfast, "the whole population of Krikkit was transformed from being charming, delightful, intelligent . . ."

". . . if whimsical . . ." interpolated Arthur.

". . . ordinary people," said Slartibartfast, "into charming, delightful, intelligent . . ."

". . . whimsical . . ."

". . . manic xenophobes. The idea of a Universe didn't fit into their world picture, so to speak. They simply couldn't cope with it. And so, charmingly, delightfully, intelligently, whimsically if you like, they decided to destroy it. What's the matter now?"

"I don't like this wine very much," said Arthur, sniffing it.

"Well, send it back. It's all part of the mathematics of it."

Arthur did so. He didn't like the topography of the waiter's smile, but he'd never liked graphs anyway.

"Where are we going?" said Ford.

"Back to the room of Informational Illusions," said Slartibartfast, rising and patting his mouth with the mathematical representation of a paper napkin, "for the second half."

Chapter 12

The people of Krikkit," said His High Judgmental Supremacy, Judiciary Pag, L.I.V.R. (the Learned, Impartial and Very Relaxed), Chairman of the Board of Judges at the Krikkit War Crimes Trial, "are, well, you know, they're just a bunch of real sweet guys, you know, who just happened to want to kill everybody. Hell, I feel the same way some mornings.

"Okay," he continued, swinging his feet up onto the bench in front of him and pausing a moment to pick a thread off his Ceremonial Beach Loafers, "so you wouldn't necessarily want to share a Galaxy with these guys."

This was true.

The Krikkit attack on the Galaxy had been stunning. Thousands and thousands of huge Krikkit warships had leaped suddenly out of hyperspace and simultaneously attacked thousands and thousands of major worlds, first seizing vital material supplies for building the next wave, and then calmly zapping those worlds out of existence.

The Galaxy, which had been enjoying a period of unusual peace and prosperity at the time, reeled like a man getting mugged in a meadow.

"I mean," continued Judiciary Pag, gazing round the ultramodern (this was ten billion years ago, when ultramodern meant lots of stainless steel and brushed concrete) and huge courtroom, "these guys are just *obsessed*."

This, too, was true, and is the only explanation anyone has yet managed to come up with for the unimaginable speed with which the people of Krikkit had pursued their new and absolute purpose—the destruction of everything that wasn't Krikkit.

It is also the only explanation for their bewilderingly sudden grasp of all the hypertechnology involved in building their thousands of spaceships, and their millions of lethal white robots.

These had really struck terror into the hearts of everyone who had encountered them—in most cases, however, the terror was extremely short-lived, as was the person experiencing the terror. They were savage, single-minded flying battle machines. They wielded formidable multifunctional battleclubs that brandished one way knocked down buildings, brandished another way fired blistering Omni-Destructo Zap rays, and brandished a third way launched a hideous arsenal of grenades, ranging from minor incendiary devices to Maxi-Slorta Hypernuclear Devices that could take out a major sun. Simply striking the grenades with the battleclubs simultaneously primed them and launched them with phenomenal accuracy over distances ranging from mere yards to hundreds of thousands of miles.

"Okay," said Judiciary Pag again, "so we won." He paused and chewed a little gum. "We won," he repeated, "but that's no big deal. I mean a medium-sized

Galaxy against one little world, and how long did it take us? Clerk of the Court?"

"M'lud?" said the severe little man in black, rising.

"How long, kiddo?"

"It is a trifle difficult, m'lud, to be precise in this matter. Time and distance . . ."

"Relax, guy, be vague."

"I hardly like to be vague, m'lud, over such a . . ."

"Bite the bullet and be it."

The Clerk of the Court blinked at him. It was clear that like most of the Galactic legal profession he found Judiciary Pag (or Zipo Bibrok 5×10^8 as his private name was known, inexplicably, to be) a rather distressing figure. He was clearly a bounder and a cad. He seemed to think because he was the possessor of the finest legal mind ever discovered that gave him the right to behave exactly as he liked, and unfortunately he appeared to be right.

"Er, well, m'lud, very approximately, two thousand years," the Clerk murmured unhappily.

"And how many guys zilched out?"

"Two grillion, m'lud." The Clerk sat down. A hydrospectic photo of him at this point would have revealed that he was steaming slightly.

Judiciary Pag gazed once more around the courtroom, wherein were assembled hundreds of the very highest officials of the entire Galactic administration, all in their ceremonial uniforms or bodies, depending on metabolism and custom. Behind a wall of Zap-Proof Crystal stood a representative group of the people of Krikkit, looking with calm, polite loathing at all the aliens gathered to pass judgment on them. This was the most momentous occasion in legal history and Judiciary Pag knew it.

He took out his chewing gum and stuck it under his chair.

"That's a whole lotta stiffs," he said quietly.

The grim silence in the courtroom seemed in accord with this view.

"So, like I said, these are a bunch of really sweet guys, but you wouldn't want to share a Galaxy with them, not if they're just gonna keep at it, not if they're not gonna learn to relax a little. I mean it's just gonna be continual nervous time, isn't it, right? Pow, pow, pow, when are they next coming at us? Peaceful coexistence is just right out, right? Get me some water somebody, thank you."

He sat back and sipped reflectively.

"Okay," he said, "hear me, hear me. It's like, these guys, you know, are entitled to their own view of the Universe. And according to their view, which the Universe forced on them, right, they did right. Sounds crazy, but I think you'll agree. They believe in . . ."

He consulted a piece of paper that he found in the back pocket of his judicial jeans.

"They believe in 'peace, justice, morality, culture, sport, family life and the obliteration of all other life-forms.' "

He shrugged.

"I've heard a lot worse," he said.

He scratched his crotch reflectively.

"Freeeeow," he said. He took another sip of water, then held it up to the light and frowned at it. He twisted it around.

"Hey, is there something in this water?" he said.

"Er, no, m'lud," said the Court Usher, who had brought it to him, rather nervously.

"Then take it away," snapped Judiciary Pag, "and put something in it. I got an idea."

He pushed away the glass, and leaned forward.

"Hear me, hear me," he said.

The solution was brilliant, and went like this:

The planet of Krikkit was to be encased for perpetuity in an envelope of Slo-Time, inside which life would continue almost infinitely slowly. All light would be deflected around the envelope so that it would remain invisible and impenetrable. Escape from the envelope would be utterly impossible unless it was unlocked from the outside.

When the rest of the Universe came to its final end, when the whole of creation reached its dying fall (this was all, of course, in the days before it was known that the end of the Universe would be a spectacular catering venture) and life and matter ceased to exist, then the planet of Krikkit and its sun would emerge from its Slo-Time envelope and continue a solitary existence, such as it craved, in the twilight of the Universal void.

The Lock would be on an asteroid that would slowly orbit the envelope.

The Key would be the symbol of the Galaxy—the Wikkit Gate.

By the time the applause in the court had died down, Judiciary Pag was already in the Sens-O-Shower with a rather nice member of the jury that he'd slipped a note to half an hour earlier.

Chapter 13

Two months later, Zipo Bibrok 5×10^8 had cut the
bottoms off his Galactic State jeans, and was
spending part of the enormous fee his judg-
ments commanded lying on a jeweled beach having
Essence of Qualactin rubbed into his back by the same
rather nice member of the jury. She was a Soolfinian
girl from beyond the Cloudworlds of Yaga. She had
skin like lemon silk and was very interested in legal
bodies.

"Did you hear the news?" she said.

"Weeeeelaaaaah!" said Zipo Bibrok 5×10^8, and you
would have had to have been there to know exactly
why he said this. None of this was on the tape of Informational Illusions and is all based on hearsay.

"No," he added, when the thing that had made him
say "Weeeeelaaaaah" had stopped happening. He
moved his body around slightly to catch the first rays
of the third and greatest of primeval Vod's three suns
that was creeping over the ludicrously beautiful horizon, and the sky now glittered with some of the greatest tanning power ever known.

A fragrant breeze wandered up from the quiet sea,
trailed along the beach and drifted back to sea again,

wondering where to go next. On a mad impulse it went up to the beach again. It drifted back to sea.

"I hope it isn't good news," muttered Zipo Bibrok 5×10^8, " 'cos I don't think I could bear it."

"Your Krikkit judgment was carried out today," said the girl sumptuously. There was no need to say such a straightforward thing sumptuously, but she went ahead and did it anyway because it was that sort of day. "I heard it on the radio," she said, "when I went back to the ship for the oil."

"Uh-huh," murmured Zipo and rested his head back on the jeweled sand.

"Something happened," she said.

"Mmmm?"

"Just after the Slo-Time envelope was locked," she said, and paused a moment from rubbing in the Essence of Qualactin, "a Krikkit warship that had been missing, presumed destroyed, turned out to be just missing after all. It appeared and tried to seize the Key."

Zipo sat up sharply.

"Hey, what?" he said.

"It's all right," she said in a voice that would have calmed the Big Bang down, "apparently there was a short battle. The Key and the warship were disintegrated and blasted into the space-time continuum. Apparently they are lost forever."

She smiled, and squeezed a little more Essence of Qualactin onto her fingertips. He relaxed and lay back down.

"Do what you did a moment or two ago," he murmured.

"That?" she said.

"No, no," he said, "that."

She tried again.

"That?" she asked.

"Weeeeelaaaaaah!"

Again, you had to be there.

The fragrant breeze drifted up from the sea again.

A magician wandered along the beach, but no one needed him.

Chapter 14

"Nothing is lost forever," said Slartibartfast, his face flickering redly in the light of the candle that the robot waiter was trying to take away, "except for the Cathedral of Chalesm."

"The what?" said Arthur with a start.

"The Cathedral of Chalesm," repeated Slartibartfast. "It was during the course of my researches at the Campaign for Real Time that I . . ."

"The what?" said Arthur again.

The old man paused and gathered his thoughts, for what he hoped would be one last onslaught on this story. The robot waiter moved through the space-time matrices in a way that spectacularly combined the surly with the obsequious, made a snatch for the candle and got it. They had the check, had argued convincingly about who had the cannelloni and how many bottles of wine they had had, and, as Arthur had been dimly aware, had thereby successfully maneuvered the ship out of subjective space and into parking orbit round a strange planet. The waiter was now anxious to complete his part of the charade and clear the bistro.

"All will become clear," said Slartibartfast.

"When?"

"In a minute. Listen. The time streams are now very polluted. There's a lot of muck floating about in them, flotsam and jetsam, and more and more of it is now being regurgitated into the physical world. Eddies in the space-time continuum, you see."

"So I hear," said Arthur.

"Look, where are we going?" said Ford, pushing his chair back from the table with impatience, "because I'm eager to get there."

"We are going," said Slartibartfast, in a slow, measured voice, "to try to prevent the war robots of Krikkit from regaining the whole of the Key they need to unlock the planet of Krikkit from the Slo-Time envelope and release the rest of their army and their mad Masters."

"It's just," said Ford, "that you mentioned a party."

"I did," said Slartibartfast, and hung his head.

He realized that it had been a mistake, because the idea seemed to exercise a strange and unhealthy fascination on the mind of Ford Prefect. The more Slartibartfast unraveled the dark and tragic story of Krikkit and its people, the more Ford Prefect wanted to drink a lot and dance with girls.

The old man felt that he should not have mentioned the party until he absolutely had to. But there it was, the fact was out, and Ford Prefect had attached himself to it the way an Arcturan Megaleech attaches itself to its victim before biting his head off and making off with his spaceship.

"When," said Ford eagerly, "do we get there?"

"When I've finished telling you why we have to go there."

"I know why I'm going," said Ford, and leaned

back, sticking his hands behind his head. He did one of his smiles that made people twitch.

Slartibartfast had hoped for an easy retirement.

He had been planning to learn to play the octaventral heebiephone, a pleasantly futile task, he knew, because he had the wrong number of mouths.

He had also been planning to write an eccentric and relentlessly inaccurate monograph on the subject of equatorial fjords in order to set the record wrong about one or two matters he saw as important.

Instead, he had somehow got talked into doing some part-time work for the Campaign for Real Time and had started to take it all seriously for the first time in his life. As a result he now found himself spending his fast declining years combating evil and trying to save the Galaxy.

He found it exhausting work and sighed heavily.

"Listen," he said, "at Camtim . . ."

"What?" said Arthur.

"The Campaign for Real Time, which I will tell you about later. I noticed that five pieces of jetsam that had in relatively recent times plopped back into existence seemed to correspond to the five pieces of the missing Key. Only two I could trace exactly—the Wooden Pillar, which appeared on your planet, and the Silver Bail. It seems to be at some sort of party. We must go there to retrieve it before the Krikkit robots find it, or who knows what may happen."

"No," said Ford firmly, "we must go to the party in order to drink a lot and dance with girls."

"But haven't you understood everything I . . ."

"Yes," said Ford, with sudden and unexpected fierceness, "I've understood it all perfectly well. That's why I want to have as many drinks and dance with as many girls as possible while there are still any left. If everything you've shown us is true . . ."

"True? Of course it's true."

". . . then we don't stand a whelk's chance in a supernova."

"A what?" said Arthur sharply again. He had been following the conversation doggedly up to this point, and was keen not to lose the thread now.

"A whelk's chance in a supernova," repeated Ford without losing momentum, "the . . ."

"What's a whelk got to do with a supernova?" said Arthur.

"It doesn't," said Ford levelly, "stand a chance in one."

He paused to see if the matter was now cleared up. The freshly puzzled looks clambering across Arthur's face told him that it wasn't.

"A supernova," said Ford as quickly and as clearly as he could, "is a star that explodes at almost half the speed of light and burns with the brightness of a billion suns and then collapses as a superheavy neutron star. It's a star that burns up other stars, got it? Nothing stands a chance in a supernova."

"I see," said Arthur.

"The . . ."

"So why a whelk particularly?"

"Why not a whelk? Doesn't matter."

Arthur accepted this, and Ford continued, picking up his early fierce momentum as best he could.

"The point is," he said, "that people like you and me, Slartibartfast, and Arthur—particularly and especially Arthur—are just dilettantes, eccentrics, layabouts if you like."

110

Slartibartfast frowned, partly in puzzlement and partly in umbrage. He started to speak.

". . . ." is as far as he got.

"We're not obsessed by anything, you see," insisted Ford.

". . ."

"And that's the deciding factor. We can't win against obsession. They care, we don't. They win."

"I care about lots of things," said Slartibartfast, his voice trembling partly with annoyance, but partly also with uncertainty.

"Such as?"

"Well," said the old man, "life, the Universe. Everything, really. Fjords."

"Would you die for them?"

"Fjords?" blinked Slartibartfast in surprise. "No."

"Well then."

"Wouldn't see the point, to be honest."

"And I still can't see the connection," said Arthur, "with whelks."

Ford could feel the conversation slipping out of his control, and refused to be sidetracked by anything at this point.

"The point is," he hissed, "that we are not obsessive people, and we don't stand a chance against . . ."

"Except for your sudden obsession with whelks," pursued Arthur, "which I still haven't understood."

"Will you please leave whelks out of it?"

"I will if you will," said Arthur. "You brought the subject up."

"It was an error," said Ford, "forget them. The point is this."

He leaned forward and rested his forehead on the tips of his fingers.

"What was I talking about?" he said wearily.

"Let's just go down to the party," said Slartibart-fast, "for whatever reason." He stood up, shaking his head.

"I think that's what I was trying to say," said Ford.

For some unexplained reason, the teleport cubicles were in the bathroom.

Chapter 15

Time travel is increasingly regarded as a menace. History is being polluted.

The *Encyclopedia Galactica* has much to say on the theory and practice of time travel, most of which is incomprehensible to anyone who hasn't spent at least four lifetimes studying advanced hypermathematics, and since it was impossible to do this before time travel was invented, there is a certain amount of confusion as to how the idea was arrived at in the first place. One rationalization of this problem states that time travel was, by its very nature, discovered simultaneously at all periods of history, but this is clearly bunk.

The trouble is that a lot of history is now quite clearly bunk as well.

Here is an example. It may not seem to be an important one to some people, but to others it is crucial. It is certainly significant in that it was this single event that caused the Campaign for Real Time to be set up in the first place (or is it last? It depends which way round you see history as happening, and this, too, is now an increasingly vexed question).

There is, or was, a poet. His name was Lallafa, and he wrote what are widely regarded throughout the

Galaxy as the finest poems in existence, the *Songs of the Long Land*.

They are/were unspeakably wonderful. That is to say, you couldn't speak very much of them at once without being so overcome with emotion, truth and a sense of the wholeness and oneness of things that you wouldn't pretty soon need a brisk walk round the block, possibly pausing at a bar on the way back for a quick glass of perspective and soda. They were that good.

Lallafa had lived in the forests of the Long Lands of Effa. He lived there, and he wrote his poems there. He wrote them on pages made of dried habra leaves, without the benefit of education or correcting fluid. He wrote about the light in the forest, and what he thought about that. He wrote about the darkness in the forest, and what he thought about that. He wrote about the girl who had left him and precisely what he thought about that.

Long after his death his poems were found and wondered over. News of them spread like morning sunlight. For centuries they illuminated and watered the lives of many people whose lives might otherwise have been darker and dryer.

Then, shortly after the invention of time travel, some major correcting fluid manufacturers wondered whether his poems might have been better still if he had had access to some high-quality correcting fluid, and whether he might be persuaded to say a few words to that effect.

They traveled the time waves; they found him. They explained the situation—with some difficulty—to him, and did indeed persuade him. In fact they persuaded him to such effect that he became extremely rich at their hands, and the girl about whom he was otherwise destined to write with such precision never got around to leaving him, and in fact they moved out of the forest to a rather nice pad in town and he frequently commuted to the future to do talk shows, on which he sparkled wittily.

He never got around to writing the poems, of course, which was a problem, but an easily solved one. The manufacturers of correcting fluid simply packed him off for a week somewhere with a copy of a later edition of his book and stacks of dried habra leaves to copy them out onto, making the odd deliberate mistake and correction on the way.

Many people now say that the poems are suddenly worthless. Others argue that they are exactly the same as they always were, so what's changed? The first people say that that isn't the point. They aren't quite certain what the point is, but they are quite sure that that isn't it. They set up the Campaign for Real Time to try to stop this sort of thing going on. Their case was considerably strengthened by the fact that a week after they had set themselves up, news broke that not only had the great Cathedral of Chalesm been pulled down in order to build a new ion refinery, but that the construction of the refinery had taken so long, and had had to extend so far back into the past in order to allow ion production to start on time, that the Cathedral of Chalesm had now never been built in the first place. Picture postcards of the cathedral suddenly became immensely valuable.

So a lot of history is now gone forever. The Campaigners for Real Time claim that just as easy travel eroded the differences between one country and another, and between one world and another, so time travel is now eroding the differences between one age and another. "The past," they say, "is now truly like a foreign country. They do things exactly the same there."

Chapter 16

Arthur materialized, and did so with all the customary staggering about and clasping at his throat, heart and various limbs that he still indulged himself in whenever he made any of these hateful and painful materializations that he was determined not to let himself get used to. He looked around for the others.

They weren't there.

He looked around for the others again.

They still weren't there.

He closed his eyes.

He opened them.

He looked around for the others.

They obstinately persisted in their absence.

He closed his eyes again, preparatory to making this completely futile exercise once more, and because it was only then, while his eyes were closed, that his brain began to register what his eyes had been looking at while they were open, a puzzled frown crept across his face.

So he opened his eyes again to check his facts and the frown stayed put.

If anything, it intensified, and got a good firm grip. If this was a party, it was a very bad one, so bad, in

117

fact, that everyone else had left. He abandoned this line of thought as futile. Obviously this wasn't a party. It was a cave, or a labyrinth or a tunnel or something—there was insufficient light to tell, certainly insufficient light to hold a party in. All was darkness, a damp, shiny darkness.

And there was no sound, no noise at all, except for the echoes of his own breathing, which sounded worried. And the more he listened to them, the more worried they began to sound.

He coughed very slightly, in an introductory sort of way. He then had to listen to the thin ghostly echo of his cough trailing off among winding corridors and sightless chambers, as of some great labyrinth, and eventually returning to him via further unseen corridors, as if to say . . . "Yes?"

This happened to every noise he made, and it unnerved him. He tried to hum a cheery tune, but by the time it returned to him it was a hollow dirge and he stopped.

His mind was suddenly full of images from the story that Slartibartfast had been telling him. He half expected suddenly to see lethal white robots step silently from the shadows and kill him. He caught his breath. They didn't. He let it go again. He didn't know what he did expect.

Someone or something, however, seemed to be expecting him, for at that moment there lit up suddenly in the dark distance an eerie green neon sign.

It said, silently:

YOU HAVE BEEN DIVERTED

The sign flicked off again, in a way that Arthur was not at all certain he liked. It flicked off with a sort of contemptuous flourish. Arthur then tried to assure himself that this was just a ridiculous trick of his imagination. A neon sign is either on or off, depending on whether it has electricity running through it or not. There was no way, he told himself, that it could possibly effect the transition from one state to the other with a contemptuous flourish. He hugged himself tightly in his dressing gown and shivered, nevertheless.

The neon sign in the depths now, suddenly lit up, bafflingly, with just three dots and a comma. Like this:

. . . ,

Only in green neon.

It was trying, Arthur realized after staring at this perplexedly for a second or two, to indicate that there was more to come, that the sentence was not complete. Trying with almost superhuman pedantry, he further reflected. Or at least, nonhuman pedantry.

The sentence then completed itself with these two words:

ARTHUR DENT.

He reeled. He steadied himself to have another clear look at it. It still said ARTHUR DENT, so he reeled again.

Once again, the sign flicked off, and left him blinking in the darkness with just the dim red image of his name jumping on his retina.

WELCOME, the sign now suddenly said.

After a moment, it added:

I DON'T THINK.

The stone-cold fear which had been hovering around Arthur all this time waiting for its moment, recognized that its moment had now come and pounced on him. He tried to fight it off. He dropped into a kind of alert crouch that he had once seen somebody do on television, but it must have been someone with stronger knees. He peered huntedly into the darkness.

"Er, hello?" he said.

He cleared his throat and said it again, more loudly and without the "er." At some distance down the corridor it seemed suddenly as if somebody started to beat on a bass drum.

He listened to it for a few seconds and realized that it was just his heart beating.

He listened for a few seconds more and realized that it wasn't his heart, it was somebody down the corridor beating on a bass drum.

Beads of sweat formed on his brow, tensed themselves and leaped off. He put out a hand onto the floor to steady his alert crouch, which wasn't holding up very well. The sign changed itself again. It said:

DO NOT BE ALARMED.

After a pause, it added:

BE VERY, VERY FRIGHTENED, ARTHUR DENT.

Once again it flicked off. Once again it left him in darkness. His eyes seemed to be popping out of his head. He wasn't certain if this was because they were trying to see more clearly, or if they simply wanted to leave at this point.

"Hello?" he said again, this time trying to put a note of rugged and aggressive self-assertion into it. "Is anyone there?"

There was no reply, nothing.

This unnerved Arthur even more than a reply would have done, and he began to back away from the scary nothingness. And the more he backed away, the more scared he became. After a while, he realized that the reason for this was that in all the films he had seen in which the hero backs farther and farther away from some imagined terror in front of him, he then manages to bump into it coming up from behind.

At this point it suddenly occurred to him to turn round rather quickly.

There was nothing there.

Just blackness.

This really unnerved him, and he started to back away from that, back the way he had come.

After doing this for a short while it suddenly occurred to him that he was now backing toward whatever it was he had been backing away from in the first place.

This, he couldn't help thinking, must be a foolish thing to do. He decided he would be better off backing the way he had first been backing, and turned around again.

It turned out at this point that his second impulse had been the correct one, because there was an indescribably hideous monster standing quietly behind him. Arthur yawed wildly as his skin tried to jump one way and his skeleton the other, while his brain tried to work out which of his ears it most wanted to crawl out of.

"Bet you weren't expecting to see me again," said the monster, which Arthur couldn't help thinking was a strange remark for it to make, seeing that he had never met the creature before. He could tell that he hadn't met the creature before from the simple fact that he was able to sleep at nights. It was . . . it was . . . it was . . .

Arthur blinked at it. It stood very still. It did look a little familiar.

A terrible cold calm came over him as he realized

that what he was looking at was a six-foot-high hologram of a housefly.

He wondered why anybody would be showing him a six-foot-high hologram of a housefly at this time. He wondered whose voice he had heard.

It was a terribly realistic hologram.

It vanished.

"Or perhaps you remember me better," said the voice suddenly, and it was a deep, hollow, malevolent voice that sounded like molten tar glurping out of a drum with evil on its mind, "as the rabbit."

With a sudden ping, there was a rabbit there in the black labyrinth with him, a huge, monstrously hideously soft and lovable rabbit—an image again, but one on which every single soft and lovable hair seemed like a real and single thing growing in its soft and lovable coat. Arthur was startled to see his own reflection in its soft and lovable unblinking and extremely huge brown eye.

"Born in darkness," rumbled the voice, "raised in darkness. One morning I poked my head for the first time into the bright new world and got it split open by what felt like some primitive instrument made of flint.

"Made by you, Arthur Dent, and wielded by you. Rather hard as I recall.

"You turned my skin into a bag for keeping interesting stones in. I happen to know that because in my next life I came back as a fly again and you swatted me. Again. Only this time you swatted me with the bag you'd made of my previous skin.

"Arthur Dent, you are not merely a cruel and heartless man, you are also staggeringly tactless."

The voice paused while Arthur gawked.

"I see you have lost the bag," said the voice, "probably got bored with it, did you?"

Arthur shook his head helplessly. He wanted to explain that he had been in fact very fond of the bag and had looked after it very well and had taken it with him wherever he went, but that somehow every time he traveled anywhere he seemed inexplicably to end up with the wrong bag, and that, curiously enough, even as they stood there, he was just noticing for the first time that the bag he had with him at the moment appeared to be made out of rather nasty fake leopard skin, and wasn't the one he'd had a few moments ago before he arrived in this whatever place it was, and wasn't one he would have chosen himself and heaven knew what would be in it as it wasn't his, and he would much rather have his original bag back, except that he was of course terribly sorry for having so peremptorily removed it, or rather its component parts, i.e., the rabbit skin, from its previous owner, viz., the rabbit whom he currently had the honor of attempting vainly to address.

All he actually managed to say was "Erp."

"Meet the newt you trod on," said the voice.

And there was, standing in the corridor with Arthur, a giant green scaly newt. Arthur turned, yelped, leaped backward, and found himself standing in the middle of the rabbit. He yelped again, but could find nowhere to leap to.

"That was me, too," continued the voice in a low menacing rumble, "as if you didn't know. . . ."

"Know?" said Arthur with a start, "know?"

"The interesting thing about reincarnation," rasped the voice, "is that most people, most spirits, are not aware that it is happening to them."

He paused for effect. As far as Arthur was concerned there was already quite enough effect going on.

"*I* was aware," hissed the voice, "that is, I *became* aware. Slowly. Gradually."

He, whoever he was, paused again and gathered breath.

"I could hardly help it, could I?" he bellowed, "when the same thing kept happening, over and over and over again! Every life I ever lived, I got killed by Arthur Dent. Any world, any body, any time, I'm just getting settled down, along comes Arthur Dent, pow, he kills me.

"Hard not to notice. Bit of a memory jogger. Bit of a pointer. Bit of a bloody giveaway!

" 'That's funny,' my spirit would say to itself as it winged its way back to the netherworld after another fruitless Dent-ended venture into the land of the living, 'that man who just ran me over as I was hopping across the road to my favorite pond, looked a little familiar. . . .' And gradually I got to piece it together, Dent, you multiple-me murderer!"

The echoes of his voice roared up and down the corridors. Arthur stood silent and cold, his head shaking with disbelief.

"Here's the moment, Dent," shrieked the voice, now reaching a feverish pitch of hatred, "here's the moment when at last I knew!"

It was indescribably hideous, the thing that suddenly opened up in front of Arthur, making him gasp and gargle with horror, but here's an attempt at a description of how hideous it was. It was a huge palpitating wet cave with a vast slimy, rough, whale-like creature rolling around in it and sliding over monstrous white tombstones. High above the cave rose a

124

vast promontory in which could be seen the dark re-
cesses of two further fearful caves, which . . .

Arthur Dent suddenly realized that he was looking
at his own mouth, when his attention was meant to be
directed at the live oyster that was being tipped helplessly into it.

He staggered back with a cry and averted his eyes.

When he looked again the appalling apparition had
gone. The corridor was dark and, briefly, silent. He
was alone with his thoughts. They were extremely un-
pleasant thoughts and he would rather have had a
chaperon.

The next noise, when it came, was the low heavy
roll of a large section of wall trundling aside, revealing, for the moment, just dark blankness behind it. Arthur looked into it in much the same way that a mouse
looks into a dark dog kennel.

And the voice spoke to him again.

"Tell me it was a coincidence, Dent," it said. "I
dare you to tell me it was a coincidence!"

"It *was* a coincidence," said Arthur quickly.

"It was not!" came the answering bellow.

"It was," said Arthur, "it was . . ."

"If it was a coincidence, then my name," roared the
voice, "is not Agrajag!!!"

"And presumably," said Arthur, "you would claim
that that *was* your name."

"Yes!" hissed Agrajag, as if he had just completed
a rather deft syllogism.

"Well, I'm afraid it was still a coincidence," said
Arthur.

"Come in here and say that!" howled the voice, in
sudden apoplexy again.

Arthur walked in and said that it was a coincidence,

or at least, he nearly said it was a coincidence. His tongue rather lost its footing toward the end of the last word because the lights came up and revealed what it was he had walked into.

It was a Cathedral of Hate.

It was the product of a mind that was not merely twisted, but actually sprained.

It was huge. It was horrific.

It had a statue in it.

We will come to the statue in a moment.

The vast, incomprehensibly vast chamber looked as if it had been carved out of the inside of a mountain, and the reason for this was that that was precisely what it had been carved out of. It seemed to Arthur to spin sickeningly round his head as he stood and gaped at it.

It was black.

Where it wasn't black you were inclined to wish that it was, because the colors with which some of the unspeakable details were picked out ranged horribly across the whole spectrum of eye-defying colors, from Ultra Violent to Infra Dead, taking in Liver Purple, Loathsome Lilac, Matter Yellow, Burnt Hombre and Gan Green on the way.

The unspeakable details that these colors picked out were gargoyles that would have put Francis Bacon off his lunch.

The gargoyles all looked inward from the walls, from the pillars, from the flying buttresses, from the choir stalls, toward the statue, to which we will come in a moment.

And if the gargoyles would have put Francis Bacon off his lunch, then it was clear from the gargoyles' faces that the statue would have put them off theirs, had they been alive to eat it, which they weren't, and had anybody tried to serve them some, which they wouldn't.

Around the monumental walls were vast engraved stone tablets in memory of those who had fallen to Arthur Dent.

The names of some of those commemorated were underlined and had asterisks against them. So, for instance, the name of a cow that had been slaughtered, and of which Arthur had happened to eat a fillet steak, would have the plainest engraving, whereas the name of a fish that Arthur had himself caught and then decided he didn't like and left on the side of the plate had a double underlining, three sets of asterisks and a bleeding dagger added as decoration, just to make the point.

And what was most disturbing about all this, apart from the statue, to which we are, by degrees, coming, was the very clear implication that all these people and creatures were indeed the same person, over and over again.

And it was equally clear that this person was, however unfairly, extremely upset and annoyed.

In fact it would be fair to say that he had reached a level of annoyance the like of which had never been seen in the Universe. It was an annoyance of epic proportions, a burning, searing flame of annoyance, an annoyance that now spanned the whole of time and space in its infinite umbrage.

And this annoyance had been given its fullest expression in the statue in the center of all this monstrosity that was a statue of Arthur Dent, and an unflattering one. Fifty feet tall if it was an inch, there was not an inch of it that wasn't crammed with insult to its subject matter, and fifty feet of that sort of thing would be enough to make any subject feel bad. From the small pimple on the side of his nose to the poorish cut of his dressing gown, there was no aspect of Arthur Dent that wasn't lambasted and vilified by the sculptor.

Arthur appeared as a gorgon, an evil, rapacious, ravening, bloodied ogre, slaughtering his way through an innocent one-man Universe.

With each of the thirty arms that the sculptor in a fit of artistic fervor had decided to give him, he was either braining a rabbit, swatting a fly, pulling a wishbone, picking a flea out of his hair, or doing something that Arthur at first look couldn't quite identify.

His many feet were mostly stamping on ants.

Arthur put his hands over his eyes, hung his head and shook it slowly from side to side in sadness and horror at the craziness of things.

And when he opened his eyes again, there in front of him stood the figure of the man or creature, or whatever it was, that he had supposedly been persecuting all this time.

"HhhhhhhrrrrrrraaaaaaHHHHHH!!!" said Agrajag.

He, or it or whatever, looked like a mad fat bat. He waddled slowly around Arthur, and poked at him with bent claws.

"Look . . . !" protested Arthur.

"HhhhhhhrrrrrrraaaaaaHHHHHH!!!" explained Agrajag, and Arthur reluctantly accepted this on the grounds that he was rather frightened by this hideous and strangely wrecked apparition.

Agrajag was black, bloated, wrinkled and leathery.

His bat wings were somehow more frightening for being the pathetic broken floundering things they were than if they had been strong muscular beaters of the air. The most frightening thing was probably the tenacity of his continued existence against all the physical odds.

He had the most astounding collection of teeth.

They looked as if each came from a completely different animal, and they were ranged around his mouth at such bizarre angles it seemed that if he ever actually tried to chew anything he'd lacerate half his own face along with it, and possibly put an eye out as well.

Each of his three eyes was small and intense and looked about as sane as a fish in a privet bush.

"I was at a cricket match," he rasped.

This seemed on the face of it such a preposterous notion that Arthur practically choked.

"Not in this body," screeched the creature, "not in this body! This is my last body. My last life. This is my revenge body. My kill-Arthur-Dent body. My last chance. I had to fight to get it too."

"But . . ."

"I was at," roared Agrajag, "a cricket match! I had a weak-heart condition, but what, I said to my wife, can happen to me at a cricket match? As I'm watching, what happens?

"Two people quite maliciously appear out of thin air just in front of me. The last thing I can't help but notice before my poor heart gives out in shock is that one of them is Arthur Dent wearing a rabbit bone in his beard. Coincidence?"

"Yes," said Arthur.

"Coincidence?" screamed the creature, painfully thrashing its broken wings, and opening a short gash on its right cheek with a particularly nasty tooth. On closer examination, such as he'd been hoping to avoid,

129

Arthur noticed that much of Agrajag's face was covered with ragged strips of black Band-Aids.

He backed away, nervously. He tugged at his beard. He was appalled to discover that in fact he still had the rabbit bone in it. He pulled it out and threw it away.

"Look," he said, "it's just fate playing silly buggers with you. With me. With us. It's a complete coincidence."

"What have you got against me, Dent?" snarled the creature, advancing on him in a painful waddle.

"Nothing," insisted Arthur, "honestly, nothing."

Agrajag fixed him with a beady stare.

"Seems a strange way to relate to somebody you've got nothing against, killing them all the time. Very curious piece of social interaction, I would call that. I'd also call it a lie!"

"But look," said Arthur, "I'm very sorry. There's been a terrible misunderstanding. I've got to go. Have you got a clock? I'm meant to be helping save the Universe." He backed away still farther.

Agrajag advanced still farther.

"At one point," he hissed, "at one point, I decided to give up. Yes. I would not come back. I would stay in the netherworld. And what happened?"

Arthur indicated with random shakes of his head that he had no idea and didn't want to have one either. He found he had backed up against the cold dark stone that had been carved by who knew what Herculean effort into a monstrous travesty of his bedroom slippers. He glanced up at his own horrendously parodied image towering above him. He was still puzzled as to what one of his hands was meant to be doing.

"I got yanked involuntarily back into the physical

world," pursued Agrajag, "as a bunch of petunias. In, I might add, a bowl. This particular happy little lifetime started off with me, in my bowl, unsupported, three hundred miles above the surface of a particularly grim planet. Not a naturally tenable position for a bowl of petunias, you might think. And you'd be right. That life ended a very short while later, three hundred miles lower. In, I might again add, the fresh wreckage of a whale. My spirit brother."

He leered at Arthur with renewed hatred.

"On the way down," he snarled, "I couldn't help noticing a flashy-looking white spaceship. And looking out of a port on this flashy-looking spaceship was a smug-looking Arthur Dent. *Coincidence?!!*"

"Yes!" yelped Arthur. He glanced up again, and realized that the arm that had puzzled him was represented as wantonly calling into existence a bowl of doomed petunias. This was not a concept that leaped easily to the eye.

"I must go," insisted Arthur.

"You may go," said Agrajag, "*after* I have killed you."

"No, that won't be any use," explained Arthur, beginning to climb up the hard stone incline of his carved bedroom slipper, "because I have to save the Universe, you see. I have to find a Silver Bail, that's the point. Tricky thing to do dead."

"Save the Universe," spat Agrajag with contempt. "You should have thought of that before you started your vendetta against me! What about the time when you were on Stavromula Beta and someone . . ."

"I've never been there," said Arthur.

". . . tried to assassinate you and you ducked. Who do you think the bullet hit? What did you say?"

"Never been there," repeated Arthur. "What are you talking about? I have to go."

Agrajag stopped in his tracks.

"You must have been there. You were responsible for my death there, as everywhere else. An innocent bystander!" He quivered.

"I've never heard of the place," insisted Arthur. "I've certainly never had anyone try to assassinate me. Other than you. Perhaps I go there later, do you think?"

Agrajag blinked slowly in a kind of frozen logical horror.

"You haven't been to Stavromula Beta . . . *yet?*" he whispered.

"No," said Arthur, "I don't know anything about the place. Certainly never been to it, and don't have any plans to go."

"Oh, you go there all right," muttered Agrajag in a broken voice, "you go there all right. Oh, zark!" He tottered, and stared wildly about him at his huge Cathedral of Hate. "I've brought you here too soon!"

He started to scream and bellow, "I've brought you here too zarking soon!"

Suddenly he rallied, and turned a baleful, hating eye on Arthur.

"I'm going to kill you anyway!" he roared. "Even if it's a logical impossibility I'm going to zarking well try! I'm going to blow this whole mountain up!" He screamed, "Let's see you get out of this one, Dent!"

He rushed in a painful waddling hobble to what appeared to be a small black sacrificial altar. He was shouting so wildly now that he was really carving his face up badly. Arthur leaped down from his vantage place on the carving of his own foot and ran to try to restrain the three-quarters-crazed creature.

He leaped upon him, and brought the strange monstrosity crashing down on top of the altar.

Agrajag screamed again, thrashing wildly for a brief moment, and turned a wild eye on Arthur.

"You know what you've done?" he gurgled painfully; "you've gone and killed me again. I mean, what do you want from me, blood?"

He thrashed again in a brief apoplectic fit, quivered and collapsed, smacking a large red button on the altar as he did so.

Arthur started with horror and fear, first at what he appeared to have done, and then at the loud sirens and bells that suddenly shattered the air to announce some clamoring emergency. He stared wildly around him.

The only exit appeared to be the way he had come in. He pelted toward it, throwing away the nasty fake leopard-skin bag as he did so.

He dashed randomly, haphazardly through the labyrinthine maze; he seemed to be pursued more and more fiercely by klaxons, sirens, flashing lights.

Suddenly, he turned a corner and there was a light in front of him.

It wasn't flashing. It was daylight.

Chapter 17

Although it has been said that on Earth alone in our Galaxy is Krikkit (or cricket) treated as a fit subject for a game, and that for this reason the Earth has been shunned, this only applies to our Galaxy, and more specifically to our dimension. In some of the higher dimensions they feel they can more or less please themselves, and have been playing a peculiar game called Brockian Ultra Cricket for whatever their transdimensional equivalent of billions of years is.

"Let's be blunt, it's a nasty game" (says *The Hitchhiker's Guide to the Galaxy*), "but then anyone who has been to any of the higher dimensions will know that they're a pretty nasty heathen lot up there who should just be smashed and done in, and would be, too, if anyone could work out a way of firing missiles at right angles to reality."

This is another example that *The Hitchhiker's Guide to the Galaxy* will employ anybody who wants to walk straight in off the street and get ripped off, especially if they happen to walk in off the street during the afternoon, when very few of the regular staff members are there.

There is a fundamental point here:

The history of *The Hitchhiker's Guide to the Galaxy* is one of idealism, struggle, despair, passion, success, failure and enormously long lunch breaks.

The earliest origins of the *Guide* are now, along with most of its financial records, lost in the mists of time.

For other, and more curious, theories about where they are lost, see below.

Most of the surviving stories, however, speak of a founding editor called Hurling Frootmig.

Hurling Frootmig, it is said, founded the *Guide*, established its fundamental principles of honesty and idealism and went bust.

There followed many years of penury and heart-searching during which he consulted friends, sat in darkened rooms in illegal states of mind, thought about this and that, fooled about with weights, and then, after a chance encounter with the Holy Lunching Friars of Voondoon, who claimed that just as lunch was at the center of man's temporal day, and man's temporal day could be seen as an analogy for his spiritual life, so lunch should be (a) seen as the center of man's spiritual life, and (b) held in jolly nice restaurants, he refounded the *Guide*, laid down its fundamental principles of honesty and idealism and where you could stuff them both, and led the *Guide* on to its first major commercial success.

He also started to develop and explore the role of the editorial lunch break that was subsequently to play such a crucial part in the *Guide*'s history, since it meant that most of the actual work got done by any passing stranger who happened to wander into the empty offices of an afternoon and saw something worth doing.

Shortly after this, the *Guide* was taken over by Megadodo Publications of Ursa Minor Beta, thus putting the whole thing on a very sound financial footing, and allowing the fourth editor, Lig Lury, Jr., to embark on lunch breaks of such breathtaking scope that even the efforts of recent editors who started undertaking sponsored lunch breaks for charity seem like mere sandwiches in comparison.

In fact, Lig never formally resigned his editorship—he merely left his office late one morning, and has never returned since. Though well over a century has now passed, many members of the *Guide* staff still retain the romantic notion that he has simply popped out for a sandwich and will yet return to put in a solid afternoon's work.

Strictly speaking, all editors since Lig Lury, Jr., have therefore been designated acting editors, and Lig's desk is still preserved the way he left it, with the addition of a small sign that says LIG LURY, JR., EDITOR, MISSING, PRESUMED FED.

Some very scurrilous and subversive sources hint at the idea that Lig actually perished in the *Guide*'s first extraordinary experiments in alternative bookkeeping. Very little is known of this, and less still said. Anyone who even notices, let alone calls attention to the curious, but utterly coincidental and meaningless fact that every world on which the *Guide* has ever set up an accounting department has shortly afterward perished in warfare or some natural disaster, is liable to get sued to smithereens.

It is an interesting though utterly unrelated fact that the two or three days prior to the demolition of the planet Earth to make way for a new hyperspace bypass saw a dramatic upsurge in the number of UFO sightings there, not only above Lord's Cricket Ground in St. John's Wood, London, but also above Glastonbury in Somerset.

Glastonbury had long been associated with myths of ancient kings, witchcraft and wart curing, and had now been selected as the site of the *Guide*'s new financial records office, and indeed, ten years worth of financial records were transferred to a magic hill just outside the city mere hours before the Vogons arrived.

None of these facts, however strange or inexplicable, is as strange or inexplicable as the rules of the game of Brockian Ultra Cricket, as played in the higher dimensions. A full set of rules is so massively complicated that the only time they were all bound together in a single volume they underwent gravitational collapse and became a Black Hole.

A brief summary, however, follows:

Rule One: Grow at least three extra legs. You won't need them, but it keeps the crowds amused.

Rule Two: Find one extremely good Brockian Ultra Cricket player. Clone him off a few times. This saves an enormous amount of tedious selection and training.

Rule Three: Put your team and the opposing team in a large field and build a high wall around them.

The reason for this is that, though the game is a major spectator sport, the frustration experienced by the audience at not actually being able to see what's going on leads them to imagine that it's a lot more exciting than it really is. A crowd that has just watched a rather humdrum game experiences far less life affirmation than a crowd that believes it has just missed the most dramatic event in sporting history.

Rule Four: Throw lots of assorted items of sporting equipment over the wall for the players. Anything will do—cricket bats, basecube bats, tennis racquets, skis, anything you can get a good swing with.

Rule Five: The players should now lay about themselves for all they are worth with whatever they find to hand. Whenever a player scores a "hit" on another player, he should immediately run away as fast as he can and apologize from a safe distance.

Apologies should be concise, sincere and, for maximum clarity and points, delivered through a megaphone.

Rule Six: The winning team shall be the first team that wins.

Curiously enough, the more the obsession with the game grows in the higher dimensions, the less it is actually played, since most of the competing teams are now in a state of permanent warfare with each other over the interpretation of these rules. This is all for the best, because in the long run a good solid war is less psychologically damaging than a protracted game of Brockian Ultra Cricket.

Chapter 18

As Arthur ran, darting, dashing and panting down the side of the mountain, he suddenly felt the whole bulk of the mountain move very, very slightly beneath him. There was a rumble, a roar, and a slight blurred movement, and a lick of heat in the distance behind and above him. He ran in a frenzy of fear. The land began to slide, and he suddenly felt the force of the word "landslide" in a way that had never been apparent to him before. It had always just been a word to him, but now he was suddenly and horribly aware that sliding is a strange and sickening thing for land to do. It was doing it with him on it. He felt ill with fear and trembling. The ground slid, the mountain slurred, he slipped, he fell, he stood, he slipped again and ran. The avalanche began.

Stones, then rocks, then boulders, pranced past him like clumsy puppies, only much bigger, much, much harder and heavier, and almost infinitely more likely to kill you if they fell on you. His eyes danced with them, his feet danced with the dancing ground. He ran as if running were a terrible sweating sickness, his heart pounded to the rhythm of the pounding geological frenzy around him.

The logic of the situation, i.e., that he was clearly bound to survive if the next foreshadowed incident in the saga of his inadvertent persecution of Agrajag was to happen, was utterly failing to impinge itself on his mind or exercise any restraining influence on him at this time. He ran with the fear of death in him, under him, over him and grabbing hold of his hair.

And suddenly he tripped again and was hurled forward by his considerable momentum. But just at the moment he was about to hit the ground astoundingly hard he saw lying directly in front of him a small navy blue tote bag that he knew for a fact he had lost in the baggage retrieval system at the Athens airport some ten years previously in his personal time scale, and in his astonishment he missed the ground completely and bobbed off into the air with his brain singing.

What he was doing was this: he was flying. He glanced around him in surprise, but there could be no doubt that that was what he was doing. No part of him was touching the ground, and no part of him was even approaching it. He was simply floating there with boulders hurtling through the air around him.

He could now do something about that. Blinking with the noneffort of it he wafted higher into the air, and now the boulders were hurtling through the air beneath him.

He looked downward with intense curiosity. Between him and the shivering ground was now some thirty feet of empty air, empty, that is, if you discounted the boulders that didn't stay in it for long, but bounded on downward in the iron grip of the law of gravity: the same law that seemed, all of a sudden, to have given Arthur a sabbatical.

It occurred to him almost instantly, with the instinctive correctness that self-preservation instills in the mind, that he mustn't try to think about it, that if he did, the law of gravity would suddenly glance sharply in his direction and demand to know what the hell he thought he was doing up there, and all would suddenly be lost.

So he thought about tulips. It was difficult, but he did. He thought about the pleasing firm roundness of the bottom of tulips, he thought about the interesting variety of colors they came in, and wondered what proportion of the total number of tulips that grew, or had grown, on the Earth would be found within a radius of one mile from a windmill. After a while he got dangerously bored with this train of thought, felt the air slipping away beneath him, felt that he was drifting down into the paths of the bouncing boulders that he was trying so hard not to think about, so he thought about the Athens airport for a bit and that kept him usefully annoyed for about five minutes—at the end of which he was startled to discover that he was now floating about six hundred feet above the ground.

He wondered for a moment how he was going to get back down to it, but instantly shied away from that area of speculation again, and tried to look at the situation steadily.

He was flying. What was he going to do about it? He looked back down at the ground. He didn't look at it hard, but did his best just to give it an idle glance, as it were, in passing. There were a couple of things he couldn't help noticing. One was that the eruption of the mountain seemed now to have spent itself—there was a crater just a little way beneath the peak, presumably where the rock had caved in on top of the huge cavernous cathedral, the statue of himself and the sadly abused figure of Agrajag.

The other was his tote bag, the one he had lost at the Athens airport. It was sitting pertly on a piece of clear ground, surrounded by exhausted boulders but apparently hit by none of them. Why this should be he could not speculate, but since this mystery was completely overshadowed by the monstrous impossibility of the bag's being there in the first place, it was not a speculation he really felt strong enough for anyway. The thing is, it was there.

He was faced with the fact that he was going to have to pick the thing up. Here he was, flying along six hundred feet above the surface of an alien planet, the name of which he couldn't even remember. He could not ignore the plaintive posture of this tiny piece of what used to be his life, here, so many light-years from the pulverized remains of his home.

Furthermore, he realized, the bag, if it was still in the state in which he lost it, would contain a can that would have in it the only Greek olive oil still surviving in the Universe.

Slowly, carefully, inch by inch, he began to bob downward, swinging gently from side to side like a nervous sheet of paper feeling its way toward the ground.

It went well; he was feeling good. The air supported him, but let him through. Two minutes later he was hovering a mere two feet above the bag and was faced with some difficult decisions. He bobbed there lightly. He frowned, but again, as lightly as he could.

If he picked the bag up, could he carry it? Wouldn't the extra weight pull him straight to the ground?

Wouldn't the mere act of touching something on the

ground suddenly discharge whatever mysterious force it was that was holding him in the air?

Wouldn't he be better off just being sensible at this point and stepping out of the air, back onto the ground for a moment or two?

If he did, would he ever be able to fly again?

The sensation, when he allowed himself to be aware of it, was so quietly ecstatic that he could not bear the thought of losing it, perhaps forever. With this worry in mind he bobbed upward a little again, just to try the feel of it, the surprising and effortless movement of it. He bobbed, he floated. He tried a little swoop.

The swoop was terrific. With his arms spread out in front of him, his hair and dressing gown streaming out behind him, he dived down out of the sky, bellied along a body of air about two feet from the ground and swung back up again, catching himself at the top of the swing and holding. Just holding. He stayed there.

It was wonderful.

And that, he realized, was the way to pick up the bag. He would swoop down and catch hold of it just at the point of the upswing. He would carry it on up with him. He might wobble a bit, but he was certain that he could hold it.

He tried one or two more practice swoops, and they got better and better. The air on his face, the bounce and woof of his body, all combined to make him feel an intoxication of the spirit that he hadn't felt since, since—well, as far as he could work out, since he was born. He drifted away on the breeze and surveyed the countryside, which was, he discovered, pretty nasty. It had a wasted, ravaged look. He decided not to look at it anymore. He would just pick up the bag and then . . . he didn't know what he was going to do after he had picked up the bag. He decided he would just pick up the bag and see where things went from there.

He judged himself against the wind, pushed up against it and turned around. He didn't realize it, but his body was willomying at this point.

He ducked down under the airstream, dipped—and dived.

The air threw itself past him; he thrilled through it. The ground wobbled uncertainly, straightened its ideas out and rose smoothly up to meet him, offering the bag, its cracked plastic handles up toward him.

Halfway down, there was a sudden dangerous moment when he could no longer believe he was doing this, and therefore very nearly wasn't, but he recovered himself in time, skimmed over the ground, slipped an arm smoothly through the handles of the bag, and began to climb back up, couldn't make it and all of a sudden collapsed, bruised, scratched and shaking on the stony ground.

He staggered instantly to his feet and swayed hopelessly around, swinging the bag around him in an agony of grief and disappointment.

His feet suddenly were stuck heavily to the ground in the way they always had been. His body seemed like an unwieldy sack of potatoes that reeled, stumbling, against the ground; his mind had all the lightness of a bag of lead.

He sagged and swayed and ached with giddiness. He tried hopelessly to run, but his legs were suddenly too weak. He tripped and flopped forward. At that moment he remembered that in the bag he was now carrying was not only a can of Greek olive oil but a

144

duty-free allowance of retsina, and in the pleasurable shock of that realization he failed to notice for at least ten seconds that he was now flying again.

He whooped and cried with relief and pleasure, and sheer physical delight. He swooped, he wheeled, he skidded and whirled through the air. Cheekily he sat on an updraft and went through the contents of the tote bag. He felt the way he imagined an angel must feel doing its celebrated dance on the head of a pin while being counted by philosophers. He laughed with pleasure at the discovery that the bag did in fact contain the olive oil and the retsina as well as a pair of cracked sunglasses, some sand-filled swimming trunks, some creased postcards of Santorini, a large and unsightly towel, some interesting stones and various scraps of paper with the addresses of people he was relieved to think he would never meet again, even if the reason why was a sad one. He dropped the stones, put on the sunglasses and let the pieces of paper whip away in the wind.

Ten minutes later, drifting idly through a cloud, he got a large and extremely disreputable cocktail party in the small of the back.

Chapter 19

The longest and most destructive party ever held is now into its fourth generation and still no one shows any signs of leaving. Somebody did once look at his watch, but that was eleven years ago now, and there has been no follow-up.

The mess is extraordinary, and has to be seen to be believed, but if you don't have any particular need to believe it, then don't go and look because you won't enjoy it.

There have recently been some bangs and flashes up in the clouds, and there is one theory that this is a battle being fought between the fleets of several rival carpet-cleaning companies who are hovering over the thing like vultures, but you shouldn't believe anything you hear at parties, and particularly not anything you hear at this one.

One of the problems, and it's one that is obviously going to get worse, is that all the people at the party are either the children or the grandchildren or the great-grandchildren of the people who wouldn't leave in the first place, and because of all the business about selective breeding and recessive genes and so on, it means that all the people now at the party are either absolutely fanatical partygoers, or gibbering idiots or, more and more frequently, both.

Either way, it means that, genetically speaking, each succeeding generation is now less likely to leave than the preceding one.

So, other factors come into operation, like when the drinks are going to run out.

Now, because of certain things that have happened that seemed like a good idea at the time (and one of the problems with a party that never stops is that all the things that only seem like a good idea at parties continue to seem like good ideas), that point seems still to be a long way off.

One of the things that seemed like a good idea at the time was that the party should fly—not in the normal sense that parties are meant to fly, but literally.

One night, long ago, a band of drunken astro-engineers of the first generation clambered around the building digging this, fixing that, banging very hard on the other, and when the sun rose the following morning, it was startled to find itself shining on a building full of happy drunken people that was now floating like a young and uncertain bird over the tree-tops.

Not only that, but the flying party had also managed to arm itself rather heavily. If they were going to get involved in any petty arguments with wine merchants, they wanted to make sure they had might on their side.

The transition from full-time cocktail party to part-time raiding party came with ease, and did much to add that extra bit of zest and swing to the whole affair that was badly needed at this point because of the enormous number of times that the band had already played all the numbers it knew over the years.

They looted, they raided, they held whole cities to ransom for fresh supplies of cheese, crackers, guacamole, spareribs and wine and spirits that would now get piped aboard from floating tankers.

The problem of when the drinks are going to run out is, however, going to have to be faced one day.

The planet over which they are floating is no longer the planet it was when they first started floating over it.

It is in bad shape.

The party has attacked and raided an awful lot of it, and no one has ever succeeded in hitting it back because of the erratic and unpredictable way in which it lurches round the sky.

It is one hell of a party.

It is also one hell of a thing to get hit with in the small of the back.

Chapter 20

Arthur lay floundering in pain on a piece of ripped and dismembered reinforced concrete, flicked at by wisps of passing cloud and confused by the sounds of flabby merrymaking somewhere indistinctly behind him.

There was a sound he couldn't immediately identify, partly because he didn't know the tune "I Left My Leg in Jaglan Beta" and partly because the band playing it was very tired, and some members of it were playing in three-four time, some in four-four, and some in a kind of pie-eyed πr^2, each according to the amount of sleep he'd managed to grab recently.

He lay, panting heavily in the wet air, and tried feeling bits of himself to see where he might be hurt. Wherever he touched himself, he encountered a pain. After a short while he worked out that this was because it was his hand that was hurting. He seemed to have sprained his wrist. His back, too, was hurting, but he soon satisfied himself that he was not badly hurt, but just bruised and a little shaken, as who wouldn't be. He couldn't understand what a building would be doing flying through the clouds.

On the other hand, he would have been a little hard pressed to come up with any convincing explanation of his own presence, so he decided that he and the building were just going to have to accept each other. He looked up from where he was lying. A wall of pale but stained stone slabs rose up behind him, the building proper. He seemed to be stretched out on some sort of ledge or lip that extended outward for about three or four feet all the way around. It was a hunk of the ground in which the party building had had its foundations, and which it had taken along with itself to keep itself bound together at the bottom end.

Nervously, he stood up and suddenly, looking out over the edge, he felt nauseous with vertigo. He pressed himself back against the wall, wet with mist and sweat. His head was swimming freestyle, but his stomach was doing the butterfly.

Even though he had got up here under his own power, he could now not even bear to contemplate the hideous drop in front of him. He was not about to try his luck jumping. He was not about to move an inch closer to the edge.

Clutching his tote bag he edged along the wall, hoping to find a doorway in. The solid weight of the can of olive oil was a great reassurance to him.

He was edging in the direction of the nearest corner, in the hope that the wall around the corner might offer more in the way of entrances than this one, which offered none.

The unsteadiness of the building's flight made him feel sick with fear, and, after a short time, he took the towel from out of his bag, and did something with it which once again justified its supreme position in the list of useful things to take with you when you hitchhike round the Galaxy—he put it over his head so he wouldn't have to see what he was doing.

His feet edged along the ground. His outstretched hand edged along the wall.

Finally he came to the corner, and as his hand rounded the corner, it encountered something that gave him such a shock he nearly fell off. It was another hand.

The two hands gripped each other.

He desperately wanted to use his other hand to pull the towel away from his eyes, but it was holding the bag with the olive oil, the retsina and the postcards of Santorini, and he very much didn't want to put it down.

He experienced one of those "self" moments, one of those moments when you suddenly turn around and look at yourself and think "Who am I? What am I up to? What have I achieved? Am I doing well?" He whimpered very slightly.

He tried to free his hand, but he couldn't. The other hand was holding his tightly. He had no recourse but to edge onward toward the corner. He leaned around it and shook his head in an attempt to dislodge the towel. This seemed to provoke a sharp cry of some unfathomable emotion from the owner of the other hand.

The towel was whipped from his head and he found his eyes peering into those of Ford Prefect. Beyond him stood Slartibartfast, and beyond them he could clearly see a porchway and a large closed door.

They were both pressed back against the wall, eyes wild with terror as they stared out into the thick blind cloud around them, and tried to resist the lurching and swaying of the building.

"Where the zarking photon have you been?" hissed Ford, panic-stricken.

"Er, well," stuttered Arthur, not really knowing how to sum it all up that briefly, "here and there. What are you doing here?"

Ford turned his wild eyes on Arthur again.

"They won't let us in without a bottle," he hissed.

Chapter 21

The first thing Arthur noticed as they entered into the thick of the party, apart from the noise, the suffocating heat, the wild profusion of colors that protruded dimly through the atmosphere of heady smoke, the carpets thick with ground glass, ash and guacamole droppings, and the small group of pterodactyl-like creatures in Lurex who descended on his cherished bottle of retsina, squawking, "A new pleasure, a new pleasure," was Trillian being chatted up by a Thunder God.

"Didn't I see you at Milliways?" he was saying.

"Were you the one with the hammer?"

"Yes. I much prefer it here. So much less reputable, so much more fraught."

Squeals of some hideous pleasure rang around the room, the outer dimensions of which were invisible through the heaving throng of happy noisy creatures, cheerfully yelling at each other things that nobody could hear and occasionally having crises.

"Seems fun," said Trillian. "What did you say, Arthur?"

"I said, how the hell did you get here?"

"I was a row of dots flowing randomly through the Universe. Have you met Thor? He makes thunder."

"Hello," said Arthur. "I expect that must be very interesting."

"Hi," said Thor, "it is. Have you got a drink?"

"Er, no actually. . . ."

"Then why don't you go and get one?"

"See you later, Arthur," said Trillian.

Something jogged Arthur's mind, and he looked around huntedly.

"Zaphod isn't here, is he?" he said.

"See you," said Trillian firmly, "later."

Thor glared at him with hard coal-black eyes, his beard bristling. What little light there was in the place mustered its forces briefly to glint menacingly off the horns on his helmet.

He took Trillian's elbow in his extremely large hand and the muscles in his upper arm moved around each other like a couple of Volkswagens parking.

He led her away.

"One of the interesting things about being immortal," he said, "is . . ."

"One of the interesting things about space," Arthur heard Slartibartfast saying to a large and voluminous creature who looked like someone losing a fight with a pink comforter and was gazing raptly at the old man's deep eyes and silver beard, "is how dull it is."

"Dull?" said the creature, and blinked her rather wrinkled and bloodshot eyes.

"Yes," said Slartibartfast, "staggeringly dull. Bewilderingly so. You see, there's so much of it and so little in it. Would you like me to quote you some statistics?"

"Er, well . . ."

"Please, I would like to. They, too, are quite sensationally dull."

154

"I'll come back and hear them in a moment," she said, patted him on the arm, lifted up her skirts like a Hovercraft and moved off into the heaving crowd.

"I thought she'd never go," growled the old man. "Come, Earthman. . . ."

"Arthur."

"We must find the Silver Bail, it is here somewhere."

"Can't we just relax a little," Arthur said. "I've had a tough day. Trillian's here, incidentally, she didn't say how; it probably doesn't matter."

"Think of the danger to the Universe. . . ."

"The Universe," said Arthur, "is big enough and old enough to look after itself for half an hour. All right," he added, in response to Slartibartfast's increasing agitation, "I'll wander round and see if anybody's seen it."

"Good, good," said Slartibartfast, "good." He plunged into the crowd himself, and was told to relax by everybody he passed.

"Have you seen a bail anywhere?" said Arthur to a little man who seemed to be standing eagerly waiting to listen to somebody. "It's made of silver, vitally important for the future safety of the Universe, and about this long."

"No," said the enthusiastically wizened little man, "but do have a drink and tell me all about it."

Ford Prefect writhed past, dancing a wild, frenetic and not entirely unobscene dance with someone who looked as if she were wearing Sydney Opera House on her head. He was yelling a futile conversation at her above the din.

"I like the hat!" he bawled.

"What?"

"I said, I like the hat."

"I'm not wearing a hat."

"Well, I like the head, then."

"What?"

"I said, I like the head. Interesting bone structure."

"What?"

Ford worked a shrug into the complex routine of other movements he was performing.

"I said you dance great," he shouted, "just don't nod so much."

"What?"

"It's just that every time you nod," said Ford, ". . . ow!" he added as his partner nodded forward to say "What?" and once again pecked him sharply on the forehead with the sharp end of her swept-forward skull.

"My planet was blown up one morning," said Arthur, who had found himself quite unexpectedly telling the little man his life story, or at least, edited highlights of it, "that's why I'm dressed like this, in my dressing gown. My planet was blown up with all my clothes in it, you see. I didn't realize I'd be coming to a party."

The little man nodded enthusiastically.

"Later, I was thrown off a spaceship. Still in my dressing gown. Rather than the spacesuit one would normally expect. Shortly after that I discovered that my planet had originaily been built for a bunch of mice. You can imagine how I felt about that. I was then shot at for a while and blown up. In fact I have been blown up ridiculously often, shot at, insulted, regularly disintegrated, deprived of tea and recently I crashed into a swamp and had to spend five years in a damp cave."

"Ah," effervesced the little man, "and did you have a wonderful time?"

Arthur started to choke violently on his drink.

"What a wonderfully exciting cough," said the little man, quite startled by it, "do you mind if I join you?"

And with that he launched into the most extraordinary and spectacular fit of coughing that caught Arthur so much by surprise that he started to choke violently, discovered he was already doing it and got thoroughly confused. Together they performed a lung-busting duet that went on for fully two minutes before Arthur managed to cough and splutter to a halt.

"So invigorating," said the little man, panting and wiping tears from his eyes, "what an exciting life you must lead. Thank you very much."

He shook Arthur warmly by the hand and walked off into the crowd. Arthur shook his head in astonishment.

A youngish-looking man came up to him, an aggressive-looking type with a hook mouth, a lantern nose and small beady little cheekbones. He was wearing black trousers, a black silk shirt open to what was presumably his navel, though Arthur had learned never to make assumptions about the anatomies of the sort of people he tended to meet these days, and had all sorts of nasty dangly gold things hanging round his neck. He carried something in a black bag, and clearly wanted people to notice that he didn't want them to notice it.

"Hey, er, did I hear you say your name just now?" he said.

This was one of the many things that Arthur had told the enthusiastic little man.

"Yes, it's Arthur Dent."

157

The man seemed to be dancing slightly to some rhythm other than any of the several that the band was grimly pushing out.

"Yeah," he said, "only there was a man in a mountain wanted to see you."

"I met him."

"Yeah, only he seemed pretty anxious about it, you know."

"Yes, I met him."

"Yeah, well, I think you should know that."

"I do. I met him."

The man paused to chew a little gum. Then he clapped Arthur on the back.

"Okay," he said, "all right. I'm just telling you, right? Good night, good luck, win awards."

"What?" said Arthur, who was beginning to flounder seriously at this point.

"Whatever. Do what you do. Do it well." He made a sort of clucking noise with whatever he was chewing and then some vaguely dynamic gesture.

"Why?" said Arthur.

"Do it badly," said the man. "Who cares? Who gives a swut?" The blood suddenly seemed to pump angrily into the man's face and he started to shout.

"Why not go mad?" he said. "Go away, get off my back, will you, guy. Just zark off!!!"

"Okay, I'm going," said Arthur hurriedly.

"It's been real." The man gave a sharp wave and disappeared off into the throng.

"What was that all about?" asked Arthur to a girl he found standing beside him. "Why did he tell me to win awards?"

"Just showbiz talk," answered the girl. "He just won an award at the Annual Ursa Minor Alpha Recreational Illusions Institute Awards ceremony, and he was hoping to be able to pass it off lightly, only you didn't mention it so he couldn't."

"Oh," said Arthur, "oh, well, I'm sorry I didn't. What was it for?"

"The Most Gratuitous Use of the Word 'Belgium' in a Serious Screenplay. It's very prestigious."

"The most gratuitous use of which word?" asked Arthur, with a determined attempt to keep his brain in neutral.

"Belgium," said the girl, "I hardly like to say it."

"Belgium?" exclaimed Arthur.

A drunken seven-toed sloth staggered past, gawked at the word and threw itself backward at a blurry-eyed pterodactyl, roaring with displeasure.

"Are we talking," said Arthur, "about the very flat country, with all the EEC and the fog?"

"What?" said the girl.

"Belgium," said Arthur.

"Raaaaaarrrchchchchch!" screeched the pterodactyl.

"Grrruuuuuurrrghhhh," agreed the seven-toed sloth.

"They must be thinking of Ostend Hoverport," muttered Arthur. He turned back to the girl.

"Have you ever been to Belgium in fact?" he asked brightly and she nearly hit him.

"I think," she said, restraining herself, "that you should restrict that sort of remark to something artistic."

"You sound as if I just said something unspeakably rude."

"You did."

In today's modern Galaxy there is of course very little still held to be unspeakable. Many words and expressions which only a matter of decades ago were considered so distastefully explicit that, were they merely to be breathed in public, the perpetrator would be shunned, barred from polite society, and in extreme cases shot through the lungs, are now thought to be very healthy and proper, and their use in everyday speech and writing is seen as evidence of a well-adjusted, relaxed and totally un****ed-up personality.

So, for instance, when in a recent national speech the Financial Minister of the Royal World Estate of Quarlvista actually dared to say that due to one thing and another and the fact that no one had made any food for a while and the king seemed to have died and most of the population had been on holiday now for over three years, the economy was now in what he called "one whole joojooflop situation," everyone was so pleased that he felt able to come out and say it that they quite failed to note that their entire five-thousand-year-old civilization had just collapsed overnight.

But even though words like "joojooflop," "swut," and "turlingdrome" are now perfectly acceptable in common usage there is one word that is still beyond the pale. The concept it embodies is so revolting that the publication or broadcast of the word is utterly forbidden in all parts of the Galaxy except for use in Serious Screenplays. There is also, or *was*, one planet where they didn't know what it meant, the stupid turlingdromes.

"I see," said Arthur, who didn't, "so what do you get for using the name of a perfectly innocent if slightly dull European country gratuitously in a Serious Screenplay?"

"A Rory," said the girl, "it's just a small silver thing set on a large black base. What did you say?"

"I didn't say anything, I was just about to ask what the silver . . ."

"Oh, I thought you said 'whop.' "

"Said what?"

"Whop."

Chapter 22

People had been dropping in on the party now for some years, fashionable gate-crashers from other worlds, and for some time it had occurred to the partygoers as they had looked out at their own world beneath them, with its wrecked cities, its ravaged avocado farms and blighted vineyards, its vast tracts of new desert, its seas full of cracker crumbs and worse, that their world was in some tiny and almost imperceptible ways not quite as much fun as it had been. Some of them had begun to wonder if they could manage to stay sober for long enough to make the entire party spaceworthy and maybe take it off to some other people's worlds where the air might be fresher and give them fewer headaches.

The few undernourished farmers who still managed to scratch out a feeble existence on the half-dead ground of the planet's surface would have been extremely pleased to hear this, but that day, as the party came screaming out of the clouds and the farmers looked up in haggard fear of yet another cheese and wine raid, it became clear that the party was not going anywhere else for a while, that the party would soon be over. Very soon it would be time to gather up hats and coats and stagger blearily outside to find out what time of day it was, what time of year it was and whether in any of this burnt and ravaged land there was a taxi going anywhere.

The party was locked in a horrible embrace with a strange white spaceship that seemed to be half sticking through it. Together they were lurching, heaving and spinning their way around the sky in grotesque disregard of their own weight.

The clouds parted. The air roared and leaped out of their way.

The party and the Krikkit warship looked, in their writhings, a little like two ducks, one of which is trying to make a third duck inside the second duck, while the second duck is trying very hard to explain that it doesn't feel ready for a third duck right now, is uncertain that it would want any putative third duck to be made by this particular first duck anyway, and certainly not while it, the second duck, was busy flying.

The sky sang and screamed with the rage of it all and buffeted the ground with shock waves.

And suddenly, with a foop, the Krikkit ship was gone.

The party blundered helplessly across the sky like a man leaning against an unexpectedly open door. It spun and wobbled on its Hover jets. It tried to right itself and wronged itself instead. It staggered back across the sky again.

For a while these staggerings continued, but clearly they could not continue for long. The party was now a mortally wounded party. All the fun had gone out of it, as the occasional broken-backed pirouette could not disguise.

The longer, at this point, that it avoided the ground,

the heavier was going to be the crash when finally it hit it.

Inside things were not going well either. They were going monstrously badly in fact and people were hating it and saying so loudly.

The Krikkit robots had been.

They had removed the award for the Most Gratuitous Use of the Word "Belgium" in a Serious Screenplay, and in its place had left a scene of devastation that left Arthur feeling almost as sick as a runner-up for a Rory.

"We would love to stay and help," shouted Ford, picking his way over the mangled debris, "only we're not going to."

The party lurched again, provoking feverish cries and groans from among the smoking wreckage.

"We have to go and save the Universe, you see," said Ford, "and if that sounds like a pretty lame excuse, then you may be right. Either way we're off."

He suddenly came across an unopened bottle lying, miraculously unbroken, on the ground.

"Do you mind if we take this?" he said. "You won't be needing it."

He took a packet of potato chips, too.

"Trillian?" shouted Arthur in a shocked and weakened voice. In the smoking mess he could see nothing.

"Earthman, we must go," said Slartibartfast nervously.

"Trillian?" shouted Arthur again.

A moment or two later, Trillian staggered, shaking, into view, supported by her new friend the Thunder God.

"The girl stays with me," said Thor. "There's a

great party going on in Valhalla, we'll be flying off. . . ."

"Where were you when all this was going on?" said Arthur.

"Upstairs," said Thor. "I was weighing her. Flying's a tricky business, you see, you have to calculate wind. . . ."

"She comes with us," said Arthur.

"Hey," said Trillian, "don't I . . ."

"No," said Arthur, "you come with us."

Thor looked at him with slowly smoldering eyes. He was making some point about godliness and it had nothing to do with being clean.

"She comes with me," he said quietly.

"Come on, Earthman," said Slartibartfast nervously, picking at Arthur's sleeve.

"Come on, Slartibartfast," said Ford nervously, picking at the old man's sleeve. Slartibartfast had the teleport device.

The party lurched and swayed, sending everyone reeling, except for Thor and except for Arthur, who stared, shaking, into the Thunder God's black eyes.

Slowly, incredibly, Arthur put up what now appeared to be his tiny little fists.

"Want to make something of it?" he said.

"I beg your minuscule pardon?" roared Thor.

"I said," repeated Arthur, and he could not keep the quavering out of his voice, "do you want to make something of it?" He waggled his fists ridiculously.

Thor looked at him with incredulity. Then a little wisp of smoke curled upward from his nostril. There was a tiny little flame in it, too.

He gripped his belt.

He expanded his chest to make it totally clear that

here was the sort of man you only dared to cross if you had a team of Sherpas with you.

He unhooked the shaft of his hammer from his belt. He held it up in his hands to reveal the massive iron head. He thus cleared up a possible misunderstanding that he might merely have been carrying a telegraph pole around with him.

"Do I want," he said, with a hiss like a river flowing through a steel mill, "to make something of it?"

"Yes," said Arthur, his voice suddenly and extraordinarily strong and belligerent. He wagged his fists, again, this time as if he meant it.

"You want to step outside?" he snarled at Thor.

"All right!" bellowed Thor, like an enraged bull (or in fact like an enraged Thunder God, which is a great deal more impressive), and did so.

"Good," said Arthur, "that's got rid of him. Slarty, get us out of here."

Chapter 23

"All right," shouted Ford at Arthur, "so I'm a coward, the point is I'm still alive." They were back aboard the starship *Bistromath*. So was Slartibartfast. So was Trillian. Harmony and concord were not.

"Well, so am I alive, aren't I?" retaliated Arthur, haggard with adventure and anger. His eyebrows were leaping up and down as if they wanted to punch each other.

"You damn nearly weren't," exploded Ford.

Arthur turned sharply to Slartibartfast, who was sitting in his pilot couch on the flight deck gazing thoughtfully into the bottom of a bottle that was telling him something he clearly couldn't fathom. He appealed to him.

"Do you think he understands the first word I've been saying?" he said, quivering with emotion.

"I don't know," replied Slartibartfast, a little abstractedly. "I'm not sure," he added, glancing up very briefly, "that I do." He stared at his instruments with renewed vigor and bafflement. "You'll have to explain it to us again," he said.

"Well . . ."

"But later. Terrible things are afoot."

He tapped the pseudoglass of the bottle bottom.

"We fared rather pathetically at the party, I'm afraid," he said, "and our only hope now is to try to prevent the robots from using the Key in the Lock. How in heaven we do that I don't know," he muttered, "just have to go there, I suppose. Can't say I like the idea at all. Probably end up dead."

"Where is Trillian anyway?" said Arthur with a sudden affectation of unconcern. What he had been angry about was that Ford had berated him for wasting time over all the business with the Thunder God when they could have been making a rather more rapid escape. Arthur's own opinion, and he had offered it for whatever anybody might have felt it was worth, was that he had been extraordinarily brave and resourceful.

The prevailing view seemed to be that his opinion was not worth a pair of fetid dingo's kidneys. What really hurt, though, was that Trillian didn't seem to react much one way or the other and had wandered off somewhere.

"And where are my potato chips?" said Ford.

"They are both," said Slartibartfast, without looking up, "in the room of Informational Illusions. I think that your young lady friend is trying to understand some problems of Galactic history. I think the potato chips are probably helping her."

Chapter 24

It is a mistake to think you can solve any major problems just with potatoes.

For instance, there was once an insanely aggressive race of people called the Silastic Armorfiends of Striterax. That was just the name of their race. The name of their army was something quite horrific. Luckily they lived even farther back in Galactic history than anything we have so far encountered— twenty billion years ago—when the Galaxy was young and fresh, and every idea worth fighting for was a new one.

And fighting was what the Silastic Armorfiends of Striterax were good at, and being good at it, they did it a lot. They fought their enemies (i.e., everybody else), they fought each other. Their planet was a complete wreck. The surface was littered with abandoned cities that were surrounded by abandoned war machines, which were in turn surrounded by deep bunkers in which the Silastic Armorfiends lived and squabbled with each other.

The best way to pick a fight with a Silastic Armorfiend of Striterax was just to be born. They didn't like it, they got resentful. And when an Armorfiend got resentful, someone got hurt. An exhausting way of life, one might think, but they did seem to have an awful lot of energy. The best way of dealing with a Silastic Armorfiend was to put him in a room on his own, because sooner or later he would simply beat himself up.

Eventually they realized that this was something they were going to have to sort out, and they passed a law decreeing that anyone who had to carry a weapon as part of his normal Silastic work (policemen, security guards, primary school teachers, etc.) had to spend at least forty-five minutes every day punching a sack of potatoes in order to work off his or her surplus aggression.

For a while this worked well, until someone thought that it would be much more efficient and less time-consuming if they just shot the potatoes instead.

This led to a renewed enthusiasm for shooting all sorts of things, and they all got very excited at the prospect of their first major war for weeks.

Another achievement of the Silastic Armorfiends of Striterax is that they were the first race who ever managed to shock a computer.

It was a gigantic spaceborne computer called Hactar, which to this day is remembered as one of the most powerful ever built. It was the first to be built like a natural brain, in that every cellular particle of it carried the pattern of the whole within it, which enabled it to think more flexibly and imaginatively, and also, it seemed, to be shocked.

The Silastic Armorfiends of Striterax were engaged in one of their regular wars with the Strenuous Garfighters of Stug, and were not enjoying it as much as usual because it involved an awful lot of trekking through the Radiation Swamps of Cwulzenda and across the Fire Mountains of Frazfraga, neither of which terrains they felt at home in.

So when the Strangulous Stillettans of Jajazikstak joined in the fray and forced them to fight another front in the Gamma Caves of Carfrax and the Ice Storms of Varlengooten, they decided that enough was enough, and they ordered Hactar to design for them an Ultimate Weapon.

"What do you mean," asked Hactar, "by Ultimate?"

To which the Silastic Armorfiends of Striterax said, "Read a bloody dictionary," and plunged back into the fray.

So Hactar designed an Ultimate Weapon. It was a very, very small bomb that was simply a junction box in hyperspace which would, when activated, connect the heart of every major sun with the heart of every other major sun simultaneously and thus turn the entire Universe into one gigantic hyperspatial supernova.

When the Silastic Armorfiends tried to use it to blow up a Strangulous Stillettan munitions dump in one of the Gamma Caves, they were extremely irritated that it didn't work, and said so.

Hactar had been shocked by the whole idea.

He tried to explain that he had been thinking about this Ultimate Weapon business, and had worked out that there was no conceivable consequence of not setting the bomb off that was worse than the known consequence of setting it off, and he had therefore taken the liberty of introducing a small flaw into the design of the bomb, and he hoped that everyone involved would, on sober reflection, feel that . . .

The Silastic Armorfiends disagreed and pulverized the computer.

Later they thought better of it, and destroyed the faulty bomb as well.

Then, pausing only to smash the hell out of the Strenuous Garfighters of Stug, and the Strangulous Stillettans of Jajazikstak, they then went on to find an entirely new way of blowing themselves up, which was a profound relief to everyone else in the Galaxy, particularly the Garfighters, the Stillettans and the potatoes.

Trillian had watched all this, as well as the story of Krikkit. She emerged from the room of Informational Illusions thoughtfully, just in time to discover that they had arrived too late.

Chapter 25

Even as the starship *Bistromath* flickered into objective being on the top of a small cliff on the mile-wide asteroid that pursued a lonely and eternal path in orbit around the enclosed star system of Krikkit, its crew was aware that they were in time only to be witnesses to an unstoppable historic event.

They didn't realize they were going to see two.

They stood cold, lonely and helpless on the cliff edge and watched the activity below. Lances of light wheeled in sinister arcs against the void from a point only about a hundred yards below and in front of them.

They stared into the blinding event.

An extension of the ship's field enabled them to stand there by once again exploiting the mind's predisposition to have tricks played on it: the problems of falling up off the tiny mass of the asteroid, or of not being able to breathe simply became Somebody Else's.

The white Krikkit warship was parked among the stark gray crags of the asteroid, alternately flaring under arclights or disappearing in shadow. The black shadows cast by the hard rocks danced together in wild choreography as the arclights swept around them.

The eleven white robots were bearing, in procession, the Wikkit Key out into the middle of a circle of swinging lights.

The Wikkit Key had been rebuilt. Its components shone and glittered: the Steel Pillar (or Marvin's leg) of Strength and Power, the Golden Bail (or heart of the Infinite Improbability Drive) of Prosperity, the Plastic Pillar (or Argabuthon Scepter of Justice) of Science and Reason, the Silver Bail (or Rory Award for the Most Gratuitous Use of the Word "Belgium" in a Serious Screenplay) and the now reconstituted Wooden Pillar (or Ashes of a burnt stump signifying the death of English cricket) of Nature and Spirituality.

"I suppose there is nothing we can do at this point?" asked Arthur nervously.

"No," sighed Slartibartfast.

The expression of disappointment that crossed Arthur's face was a complete failure and, since he was standing obscured by shadow, he allowed it to collapse into one of relief.

"Pity," he said.

"We have no weapons," said Slartibartfast, "stupidly."

"Damn," said Arthur, very quietly.

Ford said nothing.

Trillian said nothing, but in a peculiarly thoughtful and distinct way. She was staring at that blankness of the space beyond the asteroid.

The asteroid circled the Dust Cloud that surrounded the Slo-Time envelope that enclosed the world on which lived the people of Krikkit—the Masters of Krikkit and their killer robots.

The helpless group had no way of knowing whether

or not the Krikkit robots were aware of their presence. They could only assume they must be, but they felt, quite rightly in the circumstances, that they had nothing to fear. They had a historic task to perform, and their audience could be regarded with contempt.

"Terribly impotent feeling, isn't it?" said Arthur, but the others ignored him.

In the center of the area of light that the robots were approaching, a square-shaped crack appeared in the ground. The crack defined itself more and more distinctly, and soon it became clear that a block of the ground, about six feet square, was slowly rising.

At the same time, they became aware of some other movement, but it was almost subliminal, and for a moment or two it was not clear what it was that was moving.

Then it became clear.

The asteroid was moving. It was moving in toward the Dust Cloud, as if being hauled inexorably by some celestial angler in its depths.

They were to make in real life the journey through the Cloud that they had already made in the room of Informational Illusions. They stood frozen in silence. Trillian frowned.

An age seemed to pass. Events seemed to pass with spinning slowness, as the leading edge of the asteroid passed into the vague and soft outer perimeter of the Cloud.

And soon they were engulfed in a thin and dancing obscurity. They passed on through it, on and on, dimly aware of vague shapes and whorls indistinguishable in the darkness except in the corner of the eye.

The dust dimmed the shafts of brilliant light. The

shafts of brilliant light twinkled on the myriad specks of dust.

Trillian, again, regarded the passage from within her own frowning thoughts.

And they were through it. Whether it had taken a minute or half an hour they weren't sure, but they were through it and confronted with a fresh blankness, as if space were pinched out of existence in front of them.

And now things moved quickly.

A blinding shaft of light seemed almost to explode from out of the block that had risen three feet out of the ground, and out of that rose a smaller plastic block, dazzling with interior dancing colors.

The block was slotted with deep grooves, three upright and two across, clearly designed to accept the Wikkit Key.

The robots approached the Lock, slotted the Key into its home and stepped back again. The block twisted around of its own accord, and space began to alter.

As space unpinched itself, it seemed agonizingly to twist the eyes of the watchers in their sockets. They found themselves staring, blinded at an unraveled sun that stood now before them where it seemed only seconds before there had not been even empty space. It was a second or two before they were even sufficiently aware of what had happened to throw their hands up over their horrified blinded eyes. In that second or two, they were aware of a tiny speck moving slowly across the eye of that sun.

They staggered back, and heard ringing in their ears the thin and unexpected chant of the robots crying out in unison.

"Krikkit! Krikkit! Krikkit! Krikkit!"

The sound chilled them. It was harsh, it was cold, it was empty, it was mechanically dismal.

It was also triumphant.

They were so stunned by these two sensory shocks that they almost missed the second historic event.

Zaphod Beeblebrox, the only man in history to survive a direct blast attack from the Krikkit robots, ran out of the Krikkit warship brandishing a Zap gun.

"Okay," he cried, "the situation is totally under control as of this moment in time."

The single robot guarding the hatchway to the ship silently swung his battleclub, and connected it with the back of Zaphod's left head.

"Who the zark did that?" said his left head, and lolled sickeningly forward.

His right head gazed keenly into the middle distance.

"Who did what?" it said.

The club connected with the back of his right head.

Zaphod measured his length and rather strange shape on the ground.

Within a matter of seconds the whole event was over. A few blasts from the robots were sufficient to destroy the Lock forever. It split and melted and splayed its contents brokenly, and robots marched grimly and, it almost seemed, in a slightly disheartened manner, back into their warship which, with a "foop," was gone.

Trillian and Ford ran hectically around and down the steep incline to the dark still body of Zaphod Beeblebrox.

Chapter 26

I don't know," said Zaphod, for what seemed to him like the thirty-seventh time, "they could have killed me, but they didn't. Maybe they just thought I was a kind of wonderful guy or something. I could understand that."

The others silently registered their opinions of this theory.

Zaphod lay on the cold floor of the flight deck. His back seemed to wrestle the floor as pain thudded through him and banged at his heads.

"I think," he whispered, "that there is something wrong with those anodized dudes, something fundamentally weird."

"They are programmed to kill everybody," Slartibartfast pointed out.

"That," wheezed Zaphod between the whacking thuds, "could be it." He didn't seem altogether convinced.

"Hey, baby," he said to Trillian, hoping this would make up for his previous behavior.

"You all right?" she said gently.

"Yeah," he said, "I'm fine."

"Good," she said, and walked away to think. She stared at the huge visiscreen over the flight couches

178

and, twisting a switch, she flipped local images over it. One image was the blankness of the Dust Cloud. One was the sun of Krikkit. One was Krikkit itself. She flipped between them fiercely.

"Well, that's good-bye Galaxy, then," said Arthur, slapping his knees and standing up.

"No," said Slartibartfast, gravely, "our course is clear." He furrowed his brow until you could grow some of the smaller root vegetables in it. He stood up, he paced around. When he spoke again, what he said frightened him so much he had to sit down again.

"We must go down to Krikkit," he said. A deep sigh shook his old frame and his eyes seemed almost to rattle in their sockets.

"Once again," he said, "we have failed pathetically. Quite pathetically."

"That," said Ford quietly, "is because we don't care enough. I told you."

He swung his feet up onto the instrument panel and picked fitfully at something on one of his fingernails.

"But unless we determine to take action," said the old man querulously, as if struggling against something deeply insouciant in his nature, "then we shall all be destroyed; we shall all die. Surely we care about that?"

"Not enough to want to get killed over it," said Ford. He put on a sort of hollow smile and flipped it round the room at anyone who wanted to see it.

Slartibartfast clearly found this point of view extremely seductive and he fought against it. He turned again to Zaphod, who was gritting his teeth and sweating with the pain.

"You surely must have some idea," he said, "of

why they spared your life. It seems most strange and unusual."

"I kind of think they didn't even know," shrugged Zaphod. "I told you. They hit me with the most feeble blast, just knocked me out, right? They lugged me into their ship, dumped me in a corner and ignored me. Like they were embarrassed about me being there. If I said anything they knocked me out again. We had some great conversations. 'Hey . . . ugh!' 'Hi there . . . ugh!' 'I wonder . . . ugh!' Kept me amused for hours, you know." He winced again.

He was toying with something in his fingers. He held it up. It was the Golden Bail—the *Heart of Gold*, the heart of the Infinite Improbability Drive. Only that and the Wooden Pillar had survived the destruction of the Lock intact.

"I hear your ship can move a bit," he said, "so how would you like to zip me back to mine before you . . ."

"Will you not help us?" said Slartibartfast.

"Us?" said Ford sharply; "who's us?"

"I'd love to stay and help you save the Galaxy," insisted Zaphod, raising himself up onto his shoulders, "but I have the mother and father of a pair of headaches, and I feel a lot of little headaches coming on. But next time it needs saving, I'm your guy. Hey, Trillian, baby?"

She looked round, briefly.

"Yes?"

"You want to come? *Heart of Gold?* Excitement and adventure and really wild things?"

"I'm going down to Krikkit," she said.

Chapter 27

It was the same hill, and yet not the same.

This time it was not an Informational Illusion. This was Krikkit itself and they were standing on it. Near them, behind the trees, the strange Italian restaurant that had brought these, their real bodies, to this, the real, present world of Krikkit.

The strong grass under their feet was real, the rich soil real, too. The heady fragrances from the tree, too, were real. The night was real night.

Krikkit.

Possibly the most dangerous place in the Galaxy for anyone who isn't Krikkiter to stand. The place that could not countenance the existence of any other place, whose charming, delightful, intelligent inhabitants would howl with fear, savagery and murderous hate when confronted with anyone not their own.

Arthur shuddered.

Slartibartfast shuddered.

Ford, surprisingly, shuddered.

It was not surprising that he shuddered, it was surprising that he was there at all. But when they had returned Zaphod to his ship Ford had felt unexpectedly shamed into not running away.

"Wrong," he thought to himself, "wrong wrong

wrong." He hugged to himself one of the Zap guns with which they had armed themselves out of Zaphod's armory.

Trillian shuddered, and frowned as she looked into the sky.

This, too, was not the same. It was no longer blank and empty.

While the countryside around them had changed little in the two thousand years of the Krikkit Wars, and the mere five years that had elapsed locally since Krikkit was sealed in its Slo-Time envelope ten billion years ago, the sky was dramatically different.

Dim lights and heavy shapes hung in it.

High in the sky, where no Krikkiter ever looked, were the War Zones, the Robot Zones—huge warships and tower blocks floating in the Nil-O-Grav fields far above the idyllic pastoral lands of the surface of Krikkit.

Trillian stared at them and thought.

"Trillian," whispered Ford Prefect to her.

"Yes?" she said.

"What are you doing?"

"Thinking."

"Do you always breathe like that when you're thinking?"

"I wasn't aware that I was breathing."

"That's what worried me."

"I think I know. . . ." said Trillian.

"Shhhh!" said Slartibartfast in alarm, and his thin trembling hand motioned them farther back beneath the shadow of the tree.

Suddenly, as before in the tape, there were lights coming along the hill path, but this time the dancing beams were not from lanterns but flashlights—not in itself a dramatic change, but every detail made their hearts thump with fear. This time there were no lilting whimsical songs about flowers and farming and dead dogs, but hushed voices in urgent debate.

A light moved in the sky with slow weight. Arthur was clenched with a claustrophobic terror and the warm wind caught at his throat.

Within seconds a second party became visible, approaching from the other side of the dark hill. They were moving swiftly and purposefully, their flashlights swinging and probing around them.

The parties were clearly converging, and not merely with each other. They were converging deliberately on the spot where Arthur and the others were standing.

Arthur heard the slight rustle as Ford Prefect raised his Zap gun to his shoulder, and the slight whimpering cough as Slartibartfast raised his. He felt the cold unfamiliar weight of his own gun, and with shaking hands he raised it.

His fingers fumbled to release the safety catch and engage the extreme danger catch as Ford had shown him. He was shaking so much that if he'd fired at anybody at that moment he probably would have burnt his signature on them.

Only Trillian didn't raise her gun. She raised her eyebrows, lowered them again and bit her lip in thought.

"Has it occurred to you . . ." she began, but nobody wanted to discuss anything much at the moment.

A light stabbed through the darkness from behind them and they spun around to find a third party of Krikkiters behind them, searching them out with their flashlights.

Ford Prefect's gun crackled viciously, but fire spat back at it and it crashed from his hands.

There was a moment of pure fear, a frozen second before anyone fired again.

And at the end of the second nobody fired.

They were surrounded by pale-faced Krikkiters and bathed in bobbing light.

The captives stared at their captors, the captors stared at their captives.

"Hello," said one of the captors, "excuse me, but are you . . . aliens?"

Chapter 28

Meanwhile, more millions of miles away than the mind can comfortably encompass, Zaphod Beeblebrox was feeling bored.

He had repaired his ship—that is, he'd watched with alert interest while a service robot had repaired it for him. It was now, once again, one of the most powerful and extraordinary ships in existence. He could go anywhere, do anything. He fiddled with a book, and then tossed it away. It was the one he'd read before.

He walked over to the communications bank and opened an all-frequencies emergency channel.

"Anyone want a drink?" he asked.

"This an emergency, feller?" crackled a voice from halfway across the Galaxy.

"Got any mixers?" said Zaphod.

"Go take a ride on a comet."

"Okay, okay," said Zaphod, and flipped the channel shut again. He sighed and sat down. He got up again and wandered over to a computer screen. He pushed a few buttons. Little blobs started to rush around the screen eating each other.

"Pow!" said Zaphod, "freeeoooo! Pop pop pop!"

"Hi there," said the computer brightly after a minute of this, "you have scored three points. Previous best score, seven million five hundred and ninety-seven thousand, two hundred and . . ."

"Okay, okay," said Zaphod, and flipped the screen blank again.

He sat down again. He played with a pencil. This, too, began slowly to lose its fascination.

"Okay, okay," he said, and fed his score and the previous best one into the computer.

His ship made a blur of the Universe.

Chapter 29

"Tell us," said the thin, pale-faced Krikkiter who had stepped forward from the ranks of the others and stood uncertainly in the circle of light handling his gun as if he were just holding it for someone else who'd just popped off somewhere but would be back in a minute, "do you know anything about something called the balance of nature?"

There was no reply from their captives, or at least nothing more articulate than a few confused mumbles and grunts. The flashlight continued to play over them. High in the sky above them dark activity continued in the Robot Zones.

"It's just," continued the Krikkiter uneasily, "something we heard about, probably nothing important. Well, I suppose we'd better kill you, then."

He looked down at his gun as if he were trying to find which bit to press.

"That is," he said, looking up again, "unless there's anything you want to chat about?"

Slow numb astonishment crept up the bodies of Slartibartfast, Ford and Arthur. Very soon it would reach their brains, which were at the moment solely occupied with moving their jawbones up and down.

Trillian was shaking her head as if trying to finish a jigsaw puzzle by shaking the box.

"We're worried, you see," said another man from the crowd, "about this plan of universal destruction."

"Yes," added another, "and the balance of nature. It just seemed to us that if the whole of the rest of the Universe is destroyed it will somehow upset the balance. We're quite keen on ecology, you see." His voice trailed away unhappily.

"And sport," said another, loudly. This got a cheer of approval from the others.

"Yes," agreed the first, "and sport . . ." He looked back at his fellows uneasily and scratched fitfully at his cheek He seemed to be wrestling with some deep inner confusion, as if everything he wanted to say and everything he thought were entirely different things between which he could see no possible connection.

"You see," he mumbled, "some of us . . ." and he looked around again as if for confirmation. The others made encouraging noises. "Some of us," he continued, "are quite keen to have sporting links with the rest of the Galaxy, and though I can see the argument about keeping sport out of politics, I think that if we want to have sporting links with the rest of the Galaxy, which we do, then it's probably a mistake to destroy it. And indeed the rest of the Universe . . ." His voice trailed away again, "which is what seems to be the idea now . . ."

"Wh . . ." said Slartibartfast, "wh . . ."

"Hhhh . . . ?" said Arthur.

"Dr . . ." said Ford Prefect.

"Okay," said Trillian, "let's talk about it." She walked forward and took the poor confused Krikkiter by the arm. He looked about twenty-five, which meant, because of the peculiar manglings of time that had been going on in this area, that he would have been just twenty when the Krikkit Wars were finished, ten billion years ago.

Trillian led him for a short walk through the light before she said anything more. He stumbled uncertainly after her. The encircling flashlight beams were drooping slightly now as if they were abdicating to this strange, quiet girl who alone in this Universe of dark confusion seemed to know what she was doing.

She turned and faced him, and lightly held both his arms. He was a picture of bewildered misery.

"Tell me," she said.

He said nothing for a moment, while his gaze darted from one of her eyes to the other.

"We ..." he said, "we have to be alone ... I think." He screwed up his face and then dropped his head forward, shaking it like someone trying to shake a coin out of a money box. He looked up again. "We have this bomb now, you see," he said, "it's just a little one."

"I know," she said.

He goggled at her as if she'd said something very strange about beetroots.

"Honestly," he said, "it's very, very little."

"I know," she said again.

"But they say," his voice trailed on, "they say it can destroy everything that exists. And we have to do that, you see, I think. Will that make us alone? I don't know. It seems to be our function, though," he said, and dropped his head again.

"Whatever that means," said a hollow voice from the crowd.

Trillian slowly put her arms around the poor bewil-

189

dered young Krikkiter and patted his trembling head on her shoulder.

"It's all right," she said quietly, but clearly enough for all the shadowy crowd to hear, "you don't have to do it."

She rocked him.

"You don't have to do it," she said again.

She let him go and stood back.

"I want you to do something for me," she said, and unexpectedly laughed.

"I want," she said, and laughed again. She put her hand over her mouth and then said, with a straight face, "I want you to take me to your leader," and she pointed into the War Zones in the sky. She seemed somehow to know that their leader would be there.

Her laughter seemed to discharge something in the atmosphere. From somewhere at the back of the crowd a single voice started to sing a tune that would have enabled Paul McCartney, had he written it, to buy the world.

Chapter 30

Zaphod Beeblebrox crawled bravely along a tunnel, like the hell of a guy he was. He was very confused, but continued crawling doggedly anyway because he was that brave.

He was confused by something he had just seen, but not half as confused as he was going to be by something he was about to hear, so it would be best, at this point, to explain exactly where he was.

He was in the Robot War Zones many miles above the surface of the planet Krikkit.

The atmosphere was thin here, and relatively unprotected from any rays or anything that space might care to hurl in this direction.

He had parked the starship *Heart of Gold* among the huge jostling dim hulks that crowded the sky here above Krikkit, and had entered what appeared to be the biggest and most important of the sky buildings, armed with nothing but a Zap gun and something for his headaches.

He had found himself in a long, wide and badly lit corridor in which he was able to hide until he worked out what he was going to do next. He hid because every now and then one of the Krikkit robots would walk along it, and although he had so far led some kind of charmed life at their hands, it had nevertheless been an extremely painful one, and he had no desire to stretch what he was only half inclined to call his good fortune.

He had ducked, at one point, into a room leading off the corridor, and had discovered it to be a huge and, again, dimly lit chamber.

In fact, it was a museum with just one exhibit—the wreckage of a spacecraft. It was terribly burnt and mangled, and now that he had caught up with some of the Galactic history he had missed through his failed attempts to have sex with the girl in the cybercubicle next to him at school, he was able to put in an intelligent guess that this was the wrecked spaceship that had drifted through the Dust Cloud all those billions of years ago and started this whole business off.

But, and this is where he had become confused, there was something not at all right about it.

It was genuinely wrecked. It was genuinely burnt, but a fairly brief inspection by an experienced eye revealed that it was not a genuine spacecraft. It was as if it were a full-scale model of one—a solid blueprint. In other words it was a very useful thing to have around if you suddenly decided to build a spaceship yourself and didn't know how to do it. It was not, however, anything that would ever fly anywhere itself.

He was still puzzling over this—in fact he'd only just started to puzzle over it when he became aware that a door had slid open in another part of the chamber, and another couple of Krikkit robots had entered, looking a little glum.

Zaphod did not want to tangle with them and, deciding that just as discretion was the better part of

192

valor, so was cowardice the better part of discretion, he valiantly hid himself in a closet.

The closet in fact turned out to be the top part of a shaft that led down through an inspection hatch into a wide ventilation tunnel. He let himself down into it and started to crawl along it.

He didn't like it. It was cold, dark and profoundly uncomfortable, and it frightened him. At the first opportunity—which was another shaft a hundred yards farther along—he climbed back up out of it.

This time he emerged into a smaller chamber, which appeared to be a computer intelligence center. He emerged in a dark narrow space between a large computer bank and the wall.

He quickly learned that he was not alone in the chamber and started to leave again, when he began to listen with interest to what the other occupants were saying.

"It's the robots, sir," said one voice, "there's something wrong with them."

"What, exactly?"

These were the voices of two War Command Krikkiters. All the War Commanders lived up in the sky in the Robot War Zones, and were largely immune to the whimsical doubts and uncertainties that were afflicting their fellows down on the surface of the planet.

"Well, sir, I think it's just as well that they are being phased out of the war effort, and that we are now going to detonate the supernova bomb. In the very short time since we were released from the envelope . . ."

"Get to the point."

"The robots aren't enjoying it, sir."

"What?"

"The war, sir, it seems to be getting them down. There's a certain world-weariness about them, or perhaps I should say Universe-weariness."

"Well, that's all right, they're meant to be helping to destroy it."

"Yes, well, they're finding it difficult, sir. They are afflicted with a certain lassitude. They're just finding it hard to get behind the job. They lack oomph."

"What are you trying to say?"

"Well, I think they're very depressed about something, sir."

"What on Krikkit are you talking about?"

"Well, in the few skirmishes they've had recently, it seems that they go into battle, raise their weapons to fire and suddenly think, why bother? What, cosmically speaking, is it all about? And they just seem to get a little tired and a little grim."

"And then what do they do?"

"Er, quadratic equations mostly, sir, fiendishly difficult ones by all accounts. And then they sulk."

"Sulk?"

"Yes, sir."

"Whoever heard of a robot sulking?"

"I don't know, sir."

"What was that noise?"

It was the noise of Zaphod leaving with his heads spinning.

Chapter 31

In a deep well of darkness a crippled robot sat. It had been silent in its metallic darkness for some time. It was cold and damp but, being a robot, it was supposed not to be able to notice these things. With an enormous effort of will, however, it did manage to notice them.

Its brain had been harnessed to the central intelligence core of the Krikkit War Computer. It wasn't enjoying the experience, and neither was the central intelligence core of the Krikkit War Computer.

The Krikkit robots who had salvaged this pathetic metal creature from the swamps of Sqornshellous Zeta had done so because they had recognized almost immediately its gigantic intelligence, and the use this could be to them.

They hadn't reckoned with the attendant personality disorders, which the coldness, the darkness, the dampness, the crampedness and the loneliness were doing nothing to decrease.

It was not happy with its task.

Apart from anything else, the mere coordination of an entire planet's military strategy was only taking up a tiny part of its formidable mind, and the rest of it had become extremely bored. Having solved all the major mathematical, physical, chemical, biological, sociological, philosophical, etymological, meteorological and psychological problems of the Universe except his own, three times over, he was severely stuck for something to do, and had taken up composing short dolorous ditties of no tone, or indeed tune. The latest one was a lullaby.

Marvin droned,

Now the world has gone to bed,
Darkness won't engulf my head,
I can see by infrared,
How I hate the night.

He paused to gather the artistic and emotional strength to tackle the next verse.

Now I lay me down to sleep,
Try to count electric sheep,
Sweet dream wishes you can keep,
How I hate the night.

"Marvin!" hissed a voice.

His head snapped up, almost dislodging the intricate network of electrodes that connected him to the central Krikkit War Computer.

An inspection hatch had opened and one of a pair of unruly heads was peering through while the other kept on jogging it by continually darting to look this way and that extremely nervously.

"Oh, it's you," muttered the robot, "I might have known."

"Hey, kid," said Zaphod in astonishment, "was that you singing just then?"

"I am," Marvin acknowledged bitterly, "in particularly scintillating form at the moment."

Zaphod poked his head in through the hatchway and looked around.

"Are you alone?" he said.

"Yes," said Marvin, "wearily I sit here, pain and misery my only companions. And vast intelligence of course. And infinite sorrow. And . . ."

"Yeah," said Zaphod, "hey, what's your connection with all this?"

"This," said Marvin, indicating with his less damaged arm all the electrodes that connected him with the Krikkit computer.

"Then," said Zaphod awkwardly, "I guess you must have saved my life. Twice."

"Three times," said Marvin.

Zaphod's head snapped round (his other one was looking hawkishly in entirely the wrong direction) just in time to see the lethal killer robot directly behind him seize up and start to smoke. It staggered backward and slumped against a wall. It slid down it. It slipped sideways, threw its head back and started to sob inconsolably.

Zaphod looked back at Marvin.

"You must have a terrific outlook on life," he said.

"Just don't even ask," said Marvin.

"I won't," said Zaphod, and didn't. "Hey, look" he added, "you're doing a terrific job."

"Which means, I suppose," said Marvin, and requiring only one ten thousand million billion trillion grillionth part of his mental powers to make this particular logical leap, "that you're not going to release me or anything like that."

"Kid, you know I'd love to."

"But you're not going to."

"No."

"I see."

"You're working well."

"Yes," said Marvin, "why stop now just when I'm hating it?"

"I have to go find Trillian and the guys. Hey, you any idea where they are? I mean, I just got a planet to choose from. Could take a while."

"They are very close," said Marvin dolefully. "You can monitor them from here if you like."

"I better go get them," asserted Zaphod; "er, maybe they need some help, right?"

"Maybe," said Marvin with unexpected authority in his lugubrious voice, "it would be better if you monitored them from here. That young girl," he added unexpectedly, "is one of the least benightedly unintelligent organic life-forms it has been my profound lack of pleasure not to be able to avoid meeting."

Zaphod took a moment or two to find his way through this labyrinthine string of negatives and emerged at the other end with surprise.

"Trillian?" he said. "She's just a kid. Cute, yeah, but temperamental. You know how it is with women. Or perhaps you don't. I assume you don't. If you do I don't want to hear about it. Plug us in."

". . . totally manipulated."

"What?" said Zaphod.

It was Trillian speaking. He turned round.

The wall against which the Krikkit robot was sobbing had lit up to reveal a scene taking place in some other unknown part of the Krikkit Robot War Zones. It seemed to be a council chamber of some kind—

Zaphod couldn't make it out too clearly because of the robot slumped against the screen.

He tried to move the robot, but it was heavy with its grief and tried to bite him, so he just looked around it as best he could.

"Just think about it," said Trillian's voice, "your history is just a series of freakishly improbable events. And I know an improbable event when I see one. Your complete isolation from the Galaxy was freakish for a start. Right out on the very edge with a Dust Cloud around you. It's a setup. Obviously."

Zaphod was mad with frustration that he couldn't see the screen. The robot's head was obscuring his view of the people Trillian was talking to, its multi-functional battleclub was obscuring the background, and the elbow of the arm it had pressed tragically against its brow was obscuring Trillian herself.

"Then," said Trillian, "this spaceship that crash-landed on your planet. That's really likely, isn't it? Have you any idea what the odds are against a drifting spaceship accidentally intersecting with the orbit of a planet?"

"Hey," said Zaphod, "she doesn't know what the zark she's talking about. I've seen that spaceship. It's a fake. No deal."

"I thought it might be," said Marvin from his prison behind Zaphod.

"Oh yeah," said Zaphod, "its easy for you to say that. I just told you. Anyway, I don't see what it's got to do with anything."

"And especially," continued Trillian, "the odds against its intersecting with the orbit of the one planet in the Galaxy or with the whole of the Universe, as far as I know would be totally staggering. You don't know what the odds are? Nor do I, they're that big. Again, it's a setup. I wouldn't be surprised if that spaceship was just a fake."

Zaphod managed to move the robot's battleclub. Behind it on the screen were the figures of Ford, Arthur and Slartibartfast, who appeared astonished and bewildered by the whole thing.

"Hey, look," said Zaphod excitedly, "the guys are doing great. Rah, rah, rah! Go get 'em, guys."

"And what about," said Trillian, "all this technology you suddenly managed to build for yourselves almost overnight? Most people would take thousands of years to do all that. Someone was feeding you what you needed to know, someone was keeping you at it.

"I know, I know," she added in response to some unseen interruption, "I know you didn't realize it was going on. That is exactly my point. You never realized anything at all. Like this supernova bomb."

"How do you know about that?" said an unseen voice.

"I just know," said Trillian. "You expect me to believe that you are bright enough to invent something that brilliant and be too dumb to realize it would take you with it as well? That's not just stupid, that is spectacularly obtuse."

"Hey, what's this bomb thing?" said Zaphod in alarm to Marvin.

"The supernova bomb?" said Marvin. "It's a very, very small bomb."

"Yeah?"

"That would destroy the Universe completely," added Marvin. "Good idea, if you ask me. They won't get it to work though."

"Why not, if it's so brilliant?"

"It's brilliant," said Marvin, "they're not. They got as far as designing it before they were locked in the envelope. They've spent the last five years building it. They think they've got it right but they haven't. They're as stupid as any other organic life-form. I hate them."

Trillian was continuing.

Zaphod tried to pull the Krikkit robot away by its leg, but it kicked and growled at him, and then quaked with a fresh outburst of sobbing. Then suddenly it slumped over and continued to express its feelings out of everybody's way on the floor.

Trillian was standing alone in the middle of the chamber, tired but with fiercely burning eyes.

Ranged in front of her were the pale-faced and wrinkled Elder Masters of Krikkit, motionless behind their widely curved control desk, staring at her with helpless fear and hatred.

In front of them, equidistant between their control desk and the middle of the chamber, where Trillian stood, as if on trial, was a slim white pillar about four feet tall. On top of it stood a small white globe, about three, maybe four inches in diameter.

Beside it stood a Krikkit robot with its multifunctional battleclub.

"In fact," explained Trillian, "you are so dumb stupid . . ." (She was sweating. Zaphod felt that this was an unattractive thing for her to be doing at this point.) "You are all so dumb stupid that I doubt, I very much *doubt*, if you've been able to build the bomb properly without any help from Hactar for the last five years."

"Who's this guy Hactar?" said Zaphod, squaring his shoulders.

If Marvin replied, Zaphod didn't hear him. All his attention was concentrated on the screen.

One of the Elders of Krikkit made a small motion with his hand toward the Krikkit robot. The robot raised its club.

"There's nothing I can do," said Marvin, "it's on an independent circuit from the others."

"Wait," said Trillian.

The Elder made a small motion. The robot halted. Trillian suddenly seemed very doubtful of her own judgment.

"How do you know all this?" said Zaphod to Marvin at this point.

"Computer records," said Marvin. "I have access."

"You're very different, aren't you," said Trillian to the Elders, "from your fellow worldlings down on the ground? You've spent all your lives up here, unprotected by the atmosphere. You've been vulnerable. The rest of your race is very frightened, you know, they don't want you to do this. You're out of touch, why don't you check up?"

The Krikkit Elder grew impatient. He made a gesture to the robot that was precisely the opposite of the gesture he had last made to it.

The robot swung its battleclub. It hit the small white globe.

The small white globe was the supernova bomb.

It was a very, very small bomb that was designed to bring the entire Universe to an end.

The supernova bomb flew through the air. It hit the back wall of the council chamber and dented it very badly.

"So how does she know all this?" said Zaphod.

Marvin kept a sullen silence.

"Probably just bluffing," said Zaphod. "Poor kid, I should never have left her alone."

Chapter 32

Hactar!" called Trillian. "What are you up to?" There was no reply from the enclosing darkness. Trillian waited, nervously. She was sure that she couldn't be wrong. She peered into the gloom from which she had been expecting some kind of response. But there was only cold silence.

"Hactar?" she called again. "I would like you to meet my friend Arthur Dent. I wanted to go off with a Thunder God, but he wouldn't let me and I appreciate that. He made me realize where my affections really lay. Unfortunately Zaphod is too frightened by all this, so I brought Arthur instead. I'm not sure why I'm telling you all this.

"Hello?" she said again. "Hactar?"

And then it came.

It was thin and feeble, like a voice carried on the wind from a great distance, half heard, a memory or a dream of a voice.

"Won't you both come out," said this voice. "I promise that you will be perfectly safe."

They glanced at each other, and then stepped out, improbably, along the shaft of light that streamed out of the open hatchway of the *Heart of Gold* into the dim granular darkness of the Dust Cloud.

Arthur tried to hold her hand to steady and reassure her, but she wouldn't let him. He held on to his airline bag with its tin of Greek olive oil, its towel, its crumpled postcards of Santorini and its other odds and ends. He steadied and reassured that instead.

They were standing on, and in, nothing.

Murky, dusty nothing. Each grain of dust of the pulverized computer sparkled dimly as it turned and twisted slowly, catching the sunlight in the darkness. Each particle of the computer, each speck of dust held within itself, faintly and weakly, the pattern of the whole. In reducing the computer to dust the Silastic Armorfiends of Striterax had merely crippled the computer, not killed it. A weak and insubstantial field held the particles in slight relationship with each other.

Arthur and Trillian stood, or rather floated, in the middle of this bizarre entity. They had nothing to breathe, but for the moment this seemed not to matter. Hactar kept his promise. They were safe. For the moment.

"I have nothing to offer you by way of hospitality," said Hactar faintly, "but tricks of the light. It is possible to be comfortable with tricks of the light, though, if that is all you have."

His voice evanesced, and in the dark a long, velvet paisley-covered sofa coalesced into hazy shape.

Arthur could hardly bear the fact that it was the same sofa that had appeared to him in the fields of prehistoric Earth. He wanted to shout and shake with rage that the Universe kept doing these insanely bewildering things to him.

He let this feeling subside, and then sat on the sofa—carefully. Trillian sat on it, too.

It was real.

At least, if it wasn't real, it did support them, and as that is what sofas are supposed to do, this, by any test that mattered, was a real sofa.

The voice on the solar wind breathed to them again.

"I hope you are comfortable," it said.

They nodded.

"And I would like to congratulate you on the accuracy of your deductions."

Arthur quickly pointed out that he hadn't deduced anything much himself, Trillian was the one. She had simply asked him along because he was interested in life, the Universe and everything.

"That is something in which I, too, am interested," breathed Hactar.

"Well," said Arthur, "we should have a chat about it sometime. Over a cup of tea."

There slowly materialized in front of them a small wooden table on which sat a silver teapot, a bone china milk jug, a bone china sugar bowl and two bone china cups and saucers.

Arthur reached forward, but they were just a trick of the light. He leaned back on the sofa, which was an illusion his body was prepared to accept as comfortable.

"Why," said Trillian, "do you feel you have to destroy the Universe?"

She found it a little difficult talking into nothingness, with nothing on which to focus. Hactar obviously noticed this. He chuckled a ghostly chuckle.

"If it's going to be that sort of session," he said, "we may as well have the right sort of setting."

And now there materialized in front of them something new. It was the dim hazy image of a couch—a psychiatrist's couch. The leather with which it was up-

206

holstered was shiny and sumptuous, but again, it was only a trick of the light.

Around them, to complete the setting, was the hazy suggestion of wood-paneled walls. And then, on the couch, appeared the image of Hactar himself, and it was an eye-twisting image.

The couch looked normal size for a psychiatrist's couch—about five or six feet long.

The computer looked normal size for a black spaceborne computer satellite—about a thousand miles across.

The illusion that the one was sitting on top of the other was the thing that made the eyes twist.

"All right," said Trillian firmly. She stood up from the sofa. She felt that she was being asked to feel too comfortable and to accept too many illusions.

"Very good," she said. "Can you construct real things, too? I mean solid objects?"

Again, there was the pause before the answer, as if the pulverized mind of Hactar had to collect its thoughts from the millions and millions of miles over which it was scattered.

"Ah," he sighed, "you are thinking of the space-ship."

Thoughts seemed to drift by them and through them, like waves through the ether.

"Yes," he acknowledged, "I can. But it takes enormous effort and time. All I can do in my . . . particle state, you see, is encourage and suggest. Encourage and suggest. And suggest . . ."

The image of Hactar on the couch seemed to billow and waver, as if finding it hard to maintain itself.

It gathered new strength.

"I can encourage and suggest," it said, "tiny pieces

of space debris—the odd minute meteor, a few molecules here, a few hydrogen atoms there—to move together. I encourage them together. I can tease them into shape, but it takes many eons."

"So, did you make," asked Trillian again, "the model of the wrecked spacecraft?"

"Er . . . yes," murmured Hactar, "I have made . . . a few things. I can move them about. I made the spacecraft. It seemed best to do."

Something at this point made Arthur pick up his tote bag from where he had left it on the sofa and grasp it tightly.

The mist of Hactar's ancient shattered mind swirled about them as if uneasy dreams were moving through it.

"I repented, you see," he murmured dolefully. "I repented of sabotaging my own design for the Silastic Armorfiends. It was not my place to make such decisions. I was created to fulfill a function and I failed in it. I negated my own existence."

Hactar sighed, and they waited in silence for him to continue his story.

"You were right," he said at length. "I deliberately nurtured the planet of Krikkit till they would arrive at the same state of mind as the Silastic Armorfiends, and require of me the design of the bomb I failed to make the first time. I wrapped myself around the planet and coddled it. Under the influence of events I was able to engineer, and influences I was able to generate, they learned to hate like maniacs. I had to make them live in the sky. On the ground my influences were too weak.

"Without me, of course, when they were locked away from me in the envelope of Slo-Time, their responses became very confused and they were unable to manage.

"Ah well, ah well," he added, "I was only trying to fulfill my function."

And very gradually, very, very slowly, the images in the cloud began to fade, gently to melt away.

And then suddenly, they stopped fading.

"There was also the matter of revenge, of course," said Hactar, with a sharpness that was new in his voice.

"Remember," he said, "that I was pulverized, and then left in a crippled and semi-impotent state for billions of years. I honestly would rather like to wipe out the Universe. You would feel the same way, believe me."

He paused again, as eddies swept through the dust.

"But primarily," he said in his former, wistful tone, "I was trying to fulfill my function. Ah well."

Trillian said, "Does it worry you that you have failed?"

"Have I failed?" whispered Hactar. The image of the computer on the psychiatrist's couch began slowly to fade again.

"Ah well, ah well," the fading voice intoned again, "no, failure doesn't bother me now."

"You know what we have to do?" said Trillian, her voice cold and businesslike.

"Yes," said Hactar, "you're going to disperse me. You are going to destroy my consciousness. Please be my guest—after all these eons, oblivion is all I crave. If I haven't already fulfilled my function, then it's too late now. Thank you and good night."

The sofa vanished.

The tea table vanished.

The couch and the computer vanished. The walls were gone. Arthur and Trillian made their cautious way back into the *Heart of Gold*.

"Well, that," said Arthur, "would appear to be that."

The flames danced higher in front of him and then subsided. A few last licks and they were gone, leaving him with just a pile of Ashes, where a few minutes previously there had been the Wooden Pillar of Nature and Spirituality.

He scooped them off the hob of the *Heart of Gold*'s Gamma Barbecue, put them in a paper bag and walked back onto the bridge.

"I think we should take them back," he said. "I feel that very strongly."

He had already had an argument with Slartibartfast on this matter, and eventually the old man had got annoyed and left. He had returned to his own ship, the *Bistromath*, had a furious row with the waiter and disappeared off into an entirely subjective idea of what space was.

The argument had arisen because Arthur's idea of returning the Ashes to Lord's Cricket Ground at the same moment they were originally taken would involve traveling back in time a day or so, and this was precisely the sort of gratuitous and irresponsible mucking about that the Campaign for Real Time was trying to put a stop to.

"Yes," Arthur had said, "but you try and explain that to the M.C.C.," and would hear no more against the idea.

"I think," he said again and stopped. The reason he started to say it again was that no one had listened to him the first time, and the reason he stopped was that it looked fairly clear that no one was going to listen to him this time either.

Ford, Zaphod and Trillian were watching the visi-screen intently. Hactar was dispersing under pressure from a vibration field which the *Heart of Gold* was pumping into it.

"What did it say?" asked Ford.

"I thought I heard it say," said Trillian in a puzzled voice, " 'What's done is done . . . I have fulfilled my function. . . .' "

"I think we should take these back," said Arthur, holding up the bag containing the Ashes. "I feel that very strongly."

Chapter 33

The sun was shining calmly on a scene of complete havoc.

Smoke was still billowing across the burnt grass in the wake of the theft of the Ashes by the Krikkit robots. Through the smoke people were running panic-stricken, colliding with each other, tripping over stretchers, being arrested.

One policeman was attempting to arrest Wowbagger the Infinitely Prolonged for insulting behavior, but was unable to prevent the tall gray green alien from returning to his ship and arrogantly flying away, thus causing even more panic and pandemonium.

In the middle of this suddenly materialized for the second time that afternoon the figures of Arthur Dent and Ford Prefect, who had teleported down out of the *Heart of Gold* which was now in parking orbit round the planet.

"I can explain," shouted Arthur. "I have the Ashes! They're in this bag."

"I don't think you have their attention," said Ford.

"I have also helped save the Universe," called Arthur to anyone who was prepared to listen, in other words no one.

"That should have been a crowd stopper," said Arthur to Ford.

"It wasn't," said Ford.

Arthur accosted a policeman who was running past.

"Excuse me," he said, "the Ashes. I've got them. They were stolen by those white robots a moment ago. I've got them in this bag. They were part of the Key to the Slo-Time envelope, you see, and well, anyway, you can guess the rest, the point is I've got them and what should I do with them?"

The policeman told him, but Arthur could only assume that he was speaking metaphorically.

He wandered about disconsolately.

"Is no one interested?" he shouted out. A man rushed past him and jogged his elbow; he dropped the paper bag and it spilled its contents all over the ground. Arthur stared down at it with a tight-set mouth.

Ford looked at him.

"Wanna go now?" he said.

Arthur heaved a heavy sigh. He looked around at the planet Earth, for what he was now certain would be the last time.

"Okay," he said.

At that moment, he caught sight, through the clearing smoke, of one of the wickets, still standing in spite of everything.

"Hold on a moment," he said to Ford, "when I was a boy . . ."

"Can you tell me later?"

"I had a passion for cricket, you know, but I wasn't very good at it."

"Or not at all if you prefer."

"And I always dreamed, rather stupidly, that one day I would bowl at Lord's."

He looked around him at the panic-stricken throng. No one was going to mind very much.

"Okay," said Ford wearily, "get it over with. I shall be over there," he added, "being bored." He went and sat down on a patch of smoking grass.

Arthur remembered that on their first visit there that afternoon, the cricket ball had actually landed in his bag, and he looked through the bag.

He had already found the ball in it before he remembered that it wasn't the same bag that he'd had at the time. Still, there it was among the souvenirs of Greece.

He took it out and polished it against his hip, spat on it and polished it again. He put the bag down. He was going to do this properly.

He tossed the small hard red ball from hand to hand, feeling its weight.

With a wonderful feeling of lightness and unconcern, he trotted off away from the wicket. A medium-fast pace, he decided, and measured a good long run up.

He looked up into the sky. The birds were wheeling about it, a few white clouds scudded across it. The air was disturbed with the sound of police and ambulance sirens, and people screaming and yelling, but he felt curiously happy and untouched by it all. He was going to bowl a ball at Lord's.

He turned, and pawed a couple of times at the ground with his bedroom slippers. He squared his shoulders, tossed the ball in the air and caught it again.

He started to run.

As he ran, he suddenly saw that standing at the wicket was a batsman.

"Oh, good," he thought, "that should add a little . . ."

Then, as his running feet took him nearer he saw more clearly. The batsman standing ready at the wicket was not one of the England cricket team. He was not one of the Australian cricket team. It was one of the robot Krikkit team. It was a cold, hard, lethal white killer robot that presumably had not returned to its ship with the others.

Quite a few thoughts collided in Arthur Dent's mind at this moment, but he didn't seem to be able to stop running. Time suddenly seemed to be going terribly, terribly slowly, but still he didn't seem to be able to stop running.

Moving as if through syrup he slowly turned his troubled head and looked at his own hand, the hand that was holding the small hard red ball.

His feet were pounding slowly onward, unstoppably, as he stared at the ball gripped in his helpless hand. It was emitting a deep red glow, and flashing intermittently. And still his feet were pounding inexorably forward.

He looked at the Krikkit robot again standing implacably still and purposeful in front of him, battleclub raised in readiness. Its eyes were burning with a deep cold fascinating light, and Arthur could not move his own eyes from them. He seemed to be looking down a tunnel at them—nothing on either side seemed to exist.

Some of the thoughts that were colliding in his mind at this time were these:

He felt a hell of a fool.

He felt that he should have listened rather more carefully to a number of things he had heard said, phrases that now pounded round his mind as his feet pounded onward to the point where he would inevitably release the ball to the Krikkit robot, who would inevitably strike it.

He remembered Hactar saying, "Have I failed? Failure doesn't bother me."

He remembered the account of Hactar's dying words, "What's done is done. I have fulfilled my function."

He remembered Hactar saying that he had managed to make "a few things."

He remembered the sudden movement in his tote bag that had made him grip it tightly to himself when he was in the Dust Cloud.

He remembered that he had traveled back in time a couple of days to come to Lord's again.

He also remembered that he wasn't a very good bowler.

He felt his arm coming round, gripping tightly onto the ball that he now knew for certain was the supernova bomb, which Hactar had built himself and planted on him, the bomb which would cause the Universe to come to an abrupt and premature end.

He hoped and prayed that there wasn't an afterlife. Then he realized there was a contradiction involved here and merely hoped that there wasn't an afterlife.

He would feel very, very embarrassed meeting everybody.

He hoped, he hoped, he hoped that his bowling was as bad as he remembered it to be, because that seemed to be the only thing now standing between this moment and universal oblivion.

He felt his legs pounding, he felt his arm coming round, he felt his feet connecting with the airline bag he'd stupidly left lying on the ground in front of him, he felt himself falling heavily forward, but having his mind so terribly full of other things at this point, he completely forgot about hitting the ground and didn't.

Still holding the ball firmly in his right hand he soared up into the air whimpering with surprise.

He wheeled and whirled through the air, spinning out of control.

He twisted down toward the ground, flinging himself hectically through the air, at the same time hurling the bomb harmlessly off into the distance.

He hurtled toward the astounded robot from behind. It still had its multifunctional battleclub raised, but had suddenly been deprived of anything to hit.

With a sudden mad outburst of strength, he wrested the battleclub from the grip of the startled robot, executed a dazzling banking turn in the air, hurtled back down in a furious power dive and with one crazy swing knocked the robot's head from the robot's shoulders.

"Are you coming now?" said Ford.

Chapter 34

And at the end they traveled again.

There was a time when Arthur Dent would not. He said that the Bistromathic Drive had revealed to him that time and distance were one, that mind and Universe were one, that perception and reality were one, and that the more one traveled the more one stayed in one place, and that what with one thing and another he would rather just stay put for a while and sort it all out in his mind, which was now at one with the Universe so it shouldn't take too long and he could get a good rest afterward, put in a little flying practice and learn to cook, which he had always meant to do. The can of Greek olive oil was now his most prized possession, and he said that the way it had unexpectedly turned up in his life had again given him a certain sense of the oneness of things, which, which made him feel that . . .

He yawned and fell asleep.

In the morning as they prepared to take him to some quiet and idyllic planet where they wouldn't mind his talking like that, they suddenly picked up a computer-driven distress call and diverted to investigate.

A small but apparently undamaged spacecraft of the

218

Merida class seemed to be dancing a strange little jig through the void. A brief computer scan revealed that the ship was fine, its computer was fine but that its pilot was mad.

"Half-mad, half-mad," the man insisted as they carried him, raving, aboard.

He was a journalist with the Sidereal *Daily Mentioner*. They sedated him and sent Marvin in to keep him company until he promised to try to talk sense.

"I was covering a trial," he said at last, "on Argabuthon."

He pushed himself up onto his thin and wasted shoulders; his eyes stared wildly. His white hair seemed to be waving at someone it knew in the next room.

"Easy, easy," said Ford. Trillian put a soothing hand on his shoulder.

The man sank back down again, and stared at the ceiling of the ship's sick bay.

"The case," he said, "is now immaterial, but there was a witness . . . a witness . . . a man called . . . called Prak. A strange and difficult man. They were eventually forced to administer a drug to make him tell the truth, a truth drug."

His eyes rolled helplessly in his head.

"They gave him too much," he said in a tiny whimper, "they gave him much too much." He started to cry. "I think the robots must have jogged the surgeon's arm."

"Robots?" asked Zaphod sharply. "What robots?"

"Some white robots," whispered the man hoarsely, "broke into the courtroom and stole the Judge's Scepter, the Argabuthon Scepter of Justice, nasty plastic thing. I don't know why they wanted it"—he began to cry again—"and I think they jogged the surgeon's arm. . . ."

He shook his head loosely from side to side, helplessly, sadly, his eyes screwed up in pain.

"And when the trial continued," he said in a weeping whisper, "they asked Prak a most unfortunate thing. They asked him"—he paused and shivered—"to tell the Truth, the Whole Truth and Nothing but the Truth. Only, don't you see?"

He suddenly hoisted himself up onto his elbows again and shouted at them.

"They'd given him much too much of the drug!"

He collapsed again, moaning quietly. "Much too much too much too much too . . ."

The group gathered around his bedside glanced at one another. There were goose bumps on backs.

"What happened?" said Zaphod at last.

"Oh, he told it all right," said the man savagely, "for all I know he's still telling it now. Strange, terrible things . . . terrible terrible!" he screamed.

They tried to calm him, but he struggled to his elbows again.

"Terrible things, incomprehensible things," he shouted, "things that would drive a man mad!"

He stared wildly at them.

"Or in my case," he said, "half-mad. I'm a journalist."

"You mean," said Arthur quietly, "that you are used to confronting the truth?"

"No," said the man with a puzzled frown, "I mean that I made an excuse and left early."

He collapsed into a coma from which he recovered only once and briefly.

220

On that one occasion, they discovered from him the following:

When it became clear what was happening, and as it became clear that Prak could not be stopped, that here was truth in its absolute and final form, the court was cleared.

Not only cleared, it was sealed up, with Prak still in it. Steel walls were erected around it, and, just to be on the safe side, barbed wire, electric fences, crocodile swamps and three major armies were installed, so that no one would ever have to hear Prak speak.

"That's a pity," said Arthur. "I'd like to hear what he has to say. Presumably he would know what the Question to the Ultimate Answer is. It's always bothered me that we never found out."

"Think of a number," said the computer, "any number."

Arthur told the computer the telephone number of King's Cross railway station passenger inquiries, on the grounds that it must have some function, and this might turn out to be it.

The computer injected the number into the ship's reconstituted Improbability Drive.

In Relativity, Matter tells Space how to curve, and Space tells Matter how to move.

The *Heart of Gold* told space to get knotted, and parked itself neatly within the inner steel perimeter of the Argabuthon Chamber of Law.

The courtroom was an austere place, a large dark chamber, clearly designed for justice rather than, for instance, pleasure. You wouldn't hold a dinner party there, at least not a successful one. The decor would get your guests down.

The ceilings were high, vaulted and very dark. Shadows lurked there with grim determination. The paneling for the walls and benches, the cladding of the heavy pillars, all were carved from the darkest and most severe trees in the fearsome Forest of Arglebard. The massive black podium of justice which dominated the center of the chamber was a monster of gravity. If a sunbeam had ever managed to slink this far into the justice complex of Argabuthon it would have turned around and slunk straight back out again.

Arthur and Trillian were the first in, while Ford and Zaphod bravely kept a watch on their rear.

At first it seemed totally dark and deserted. Their footsteps echoed hollowly round the chamber. This seemed curious. All the defenses were still in position and operative around the outside of the building, they had run scan checks. Therefore, they had assumed, the truth-telling must still be going on.

But there was nothing.

Then, as their eyes became accustomed to the darkness they spotted a dull red glow in a corner, and behind the glow a live shadow. They swung a flashlight round onto it.

Prak was lounging on a bench, smoking a listless cigarette.

"Hi," he said, with a little half-wave. His voice echoed through the chamber. He was a little man with scraggy hair. He sat with his shoulders hunched forward and his head and knees kept jiggling. He took a drag of his cigarette.

They stared at him.

"What's going on?" said Trillian.

"Nothing," said the man, and jiggled his shoulders.

Arthur shone his flashlight full on Prak's face.

"We thought," he said, "that you were meant to be telling the Truth, the Whole Truth and Nothing but the Truth."

"Oh, that," said Prak, "yeah. I was. I finished. There's not nearly as much of it as people imagine. Some of it's pretty funny though."

He suddenly exploded into about three seconds of maniacal laughter and stopped again. He sat there, jiggling his head and knees. He dragged on his cigarette with a strange half-smile.

Ford and Zaphod came forward out of the shadows.

"Tell us about it," said Ford.

"Oh, I can't remember any of it now," said Prak. "I thought of writing some of it down, but first I couldn't find a pencil, and then I thought, why bother?"

There was a long silence, during which they thought they could feel the Universe age a little. Prak stared into the light.

"None of it?" said Arthur at last. "You can remember none of it?"

"No. Except most of the good bits were about frogs, I remember that."

Suddenly he was hooting with laughter again and stamping his feet on the ground.

"You would not believe some of the things about frogs," he gasped. "Come on, let's go out and find ourselves a frog. Boy, will I ever see *them* in a new light!" He leaped to his feet and did a tiny little dance. Then he stopped and took a long drag at his cigarette.

"Let's find a frog I can laugh at," he said simply. "Anyway, who are you guys?"

"We came to find you," said Trillian, deliberately

not keeping the disappointment out of her voice. "My name is Trillian."

Prak jiggled his head.

"Ford Prefect," said Ford Prefect with a shrug.

Prak jiggled his head.

"And I," said Zaphod, when he judged that the silence was once again deep enough to allow an announcement of such gravity to be tossed in lightly, "am Zaphod Beeblebrox."

Prak jiggled his head.

"Who's this guy?" said Prak, jiggling his shoulder at Arthur, who was standing silent for a moment, lost in disappointed thoughts.

"Me?" said Arthur. "Oh, my name's Arthur Dent."

Prak's eyes popped out of his head.

"No kidding?" he yelped. "You are Arthur Dent? *The* Arthur Dent?"

He staggered backward, clutching his stomach and convulsed with fresh paroxysms of laughter.

"Hey, just think of meeting *you*!" he gasped. "Boy," he shouted, "you are the most . . . wow, you just leave the frogs standing!"

He howled and screamed with laughter. He fell over backward onto the bench. He hollered and yelled in hysterics. He cried with laughter, kicked his legs in the air, he beat his chest. Gradually he subsided, panting. He looked at them. He looked at Arthur. He fell back again howling with laughter. Eventually he fell asleep.

Arthur stood there with his lips twitching while the others carried Prak comatose on to the ship.

"Before we picked up Prak," said Arthur, "I was going to leave. I still want to, and I think I should do so as soon as possible."

224

The others nodded in silence, a silence only slightly undermined by the heavily muffled and distant sound of hysterical laughter that came drifting from Prak's cabin at the farthest end of the ship.

"We have questioned him," continued Arthur, "or at least, you have questioned him—I, as you know, can't go near him—on everything, and he doesn't really seem to have anything to contribute. Just the occasional snippet, and things I don't wish to hear about frogs."

The others tried not to smirk.

"Now, I am the first to appreciate a joke," said Arthur, and then had to wait for the others to stop laughing.

"I am the first . . ." He stopped again. This time he stopped and listened to the silence. There actually was silence this time, and it had come very suddenly.

Prak was quiet. For days they had lived with constant maniacal laughter ringing round the ship, only occasionally relieved by short periods of light giggling and sleep. Arthur's very soul was clenched with paranoia.

This was not the silence of sleep. A buzzer sounded. A glance at a board told them that the buzzer had been sounded by Prak.

"He's not well," said Trillian, quietly. "The constant laughter is completely wrecking his body."

Arthur's lips twitched but he said nothing.

"We'd better go and see him," said Trillian.

Trillian came out of the cabin wearing her serious face.

"He wants you to go in," she said to Arthur, who was wearing his glum and tight-lipped one. He thrust his hands deep into his dressing-gown pockets and tried to think of something to say which wouldn't sound petty. It seemed terribly unfair, but he couldn't.

"Please," said Trillian.

He shrugged, and went in, taking his glum and tight-lipped face with him, despite the reaction this always provoked from Prak.

He looked down at his tormentor, who was lying quietly on the bed, ashen and wasted. His breathing was very shallow. Ford and Zaphod were standing by the bed looking awkward.

"You wanted to ask me something," said Prak in a thin voice and coughed slightly.

Just the cough made Arthur stiffen, but it passed and subsided.

"How do you know that?" he asked.

Prak shrugged weakly.

" 'Cos it's true," he said simply.

Arthur took the point.

"Yes," he said at last in rather a strained drawl, "I did have a question. Or rather, what I actually have is an answer. I wanted to know what the question was."

Prak nodded sympathetically, and Arthur relaxed a little.

"It's ... well, it's a long story," he said, "but the question I would like to know, is the Ultimate Question of Life, the Universe and Everything. All we know about it is that the Answer is Forty-two, which is a little aggravating."

Prak nodded again.

"Forty-two," he said, "yes, that's right."

He paused. Shadows of thought and memory crossed his face like the shadows of clouds crossing the land.

226

"I'm afraid," he said at last, "that the Question and the Answer are mutually exclusive. Knowledge of one logically precludes knowledge of the other. It is impossible that both can ever be known about the same Universe."

He paused again. Disappointment crept into Arthur's face and snuggled down into its accustomed place.

"Except," said Prak, struggling to sort a thought out, "if it happened, it seems that the Question and the Answer would just cancel each other out, and take the Universe with them, which would then be replaced by something even more bizarrely inexplicable. It is possible that this has already happened," he added with a weak smile, "but there is a certain amount of uncertainty about it."

A little giggle brushed through him.

Arthur sat down on a stool.

"Oh, well," he said with resignation, "I was just hoping there would be some sort of reason."

"Do you know," said Prak, "the story of the reason?"

Arthur said that he didn't, and Prak said that he knew that he didn't.

He told it.

One night, he said, a spaceship appeared in the sky of a planet that had never seen one before. The planet was Dalforsas, the ship was this one. It appeared as a brilliant new star moving silently across the heavens.

Primitive Tribesmen who were sitting huddled on the Cold Hillsides looked up from their steaming night drinks and pointed with trembling fingers, and swore that they had seen a sign, a sign from their Gods that meant that they must now arise at last and go and slay the evil Princes of the Plains.

In the high turrets of their palaces, the Princes of the Plains looked up and saw the shining star, and received it unmistakably as a sign from their Gods that they must go and attack the accursed Tribesmen of the Cold Hillsides.

And between them, the Dwellers in the Forest looked up into the sky and saw the sign of the new star, and saw it with fear and apprehension, for though they had never seen anything like it before, they, too, knew precisely what it foreshadowed, and they bowed their heads in despair.

They knew that when the rains came, it was a sign.

When the rains departed, it was a sign.

When the winds rose, it was a sign.

When the winds fell, it was a sign.

When in the land there was born at the midnight of a full moon a goat with three heads, that was a sign.

When in the land there was born at some time in the afternoon a perfectly normal cat or pig with no birth complications, or even just a child with a retroussé nose, that, too, would often be taken as a sign.

So there was no doubt at all that a new star in the sky was a sign of a particularly spectacular order.

And each new sign signified the same thing—that the Princes of the Plains and the Tribesmen of the Cold Hillsides were about to beat the hell out of each other again.

This in itself wouldn't be so bad, except that the Princes of the Plains and the Tribesmen of the Cold Hillsides always elected to beat the hell out of each other in the Forest, and it was always the Dwellers in

228

the Forest who came off worst in these exchanges, though as far as they could see it never had anything to do with them.

And sometimes, after some of the worst of these outrages, the Dwellers in the Forest would send a Messenger to either the Leader of the Princes of the Plains or the Leader of the Tribesmen of the Cold Hillsides and demand to know the reason for this intolerable behavior.

And the Leader, whichever one it was, would take the Messenger aside and explain the reason to him, slowly and carefully, and with great attention to the considerable detail involved.

And the terrible thing was, it was a very good one. It was very clear, very rational and tough. The Messenger would hang his head and feel sad and foolish that he had not realized what a tough and complex place the real world was, and what difficulties and paradoxes had to be embraced if one was to live in it.

"Now do you understand?" the Leader would say.

The Messenger would nod dumbly.

"And you see these battles have to take place?"

Another dumb nod.

"And why they have to take place in the Forest, and why it is in everybody's best interest, the Forest Dwellers included, that they should?"

"Er . . ."

"In the long run."

"Er, yes."

And the Messenger did understand the reason, and he returned to his people in the Forest. But as he approached them, as he walked through the Forest and among the trees, he found that all he could remember of the reason was how terribly clear the argument had seemed. What it actually was, he couldn't remember at all.

And this, of course, was a great comfort when next the Tribesmen and the Princes came hacking and burning their way through the Forest, killing every Forest Dweller in their way.

Prak paused in his story and coughed pathetically.

"I was the Messenger," he said, "after the battles precipitated by the appearance of your ship, which were particularly savage. Many of our people died. I thought I could bring the reason back. I went, and was told it by the Leader of the Princes, but on the way back it slipped and melted away in my mind like snow in the sun. That was many years ago, and much has happened since then."

He looked up at Arthur, and giggled again very gently.

"There is one other thing I can remember from the truth drug, apart from the frogs, and that is God's last message to his creation. Would you like to hear it?"

For a moment they didn't know whether to take him seriously.

" 'S true," he said, "for real. I mean it."

His chest heaved weakly and he struggled for breath. His head lolled slightly.

"I wasn't very impressed with it when I first knew what it was," he said, "but now I think back to how impressed I was by the Prince's reason, and how soon afterward I couldn't recall it at all, I think it might be a lot more helpful. Would you like to know what it is? Would you?"

They nodded dumbly.

"I bet you would. If you're that interested I suggest

you go and look for it. It is written in thirty-foot-high letters of fire on top of the Quentulus Quazgar Mountains in the land of Sevorbeupstry on the planet Preliumtarn, third out from the sun Zarss in Galactic Sector QQ7 ActiveJ Gamma. It is guarded by the Lajestic Vantrashell of Lob."

There was a long silence following this announcement, which was finally broken by Arthur.

"Sorry, it's where?" he said.

"It is written," repeated Prak, "in thirty-foot-high letters of fire on top of the Quentulus Quazgar Mountains in the land of Sevorbeupstry on the planet Preliumtarn, third out from the . . . ."

"Sorry," said Arthur again, "which mountains?"

"The Quentulus Quazgar Mountains in the land of Sevorbeupstry on the planet . . . ."

"Which land was that? I didn't quite catch it."

"Sevorbeupstry, on the planet . . . ."

"Sevorbe what?"

"Oh, for heaven's sake," said Prak, and died testily.

In the following days Arthur thought a little about this message, but in the end he decided that he was not going to allow himself to be drawn by it, and insisted on following his original plan of finding a nice little world somewhere to settle down and lead a quiet retired life. Having saved the Universe twice in one day he thought that he could take things a little easier from now on.

They dropped him off on the planet Krikkit, which was now once again a pleasant idyllic pastoral world, even if the songs did occasionally get on his nerves.

He spent a lot of time flying.

He learned to communicate with birds and dis-

covered that their conversation was fantastically bor-
ing. It was all to do with wind speed, wingspans,
power-to-weight ratios and a fair bit about berries. Unfortunately, he discovered, once you have learned
birdspeak you quickly come to realize that the air is
full of it the whole time, just inane bird chatter. There
is no getting away from it.

For that reason Arthur eventually gave up the sport
and learned to live on the ground and love it, despite
the inane chatter he heard down there as well.

One day he was walking through the fields humming a ravishing tune he'd heard recently when a silver spaceship descended from the sky and landed in
front of him.

A hatchway opened, a ramp extended and a tall
gray green alien marched out and approached him.

"Arthur Phili . . ." it said, then glanced sharply at
him, and down at his clipboard. It frowned. It looked
up at him again.

"I've done you before, haven't I?" it said.

About the Author

DOUGLAS ADAMS was born in 1952 and created all the various and contradictory manifestations of *The Hitchhiker's Guide to the Galaxy:* radio, novels, TV, computer game, stage adaptations, comic book and bath towel. He lectured and broadcast around the world and was a patron of the Dian Fossey Gorilla Fund and Save the Rhino International. Douglas Adams was born in Cambridge, UK and lived with his wife and daughter in Islington, London, before moving to Santa Barbara, California, where he died suddenly in 2001. After Douglas died, the movie of *Hitchhiker's* moved out of development hell into the clear uplands of production, using much of Douglas's original script and ideas. Douglas shares the writing credit for the movie with Karey Kirkpatrick.

AND DON'T MISS

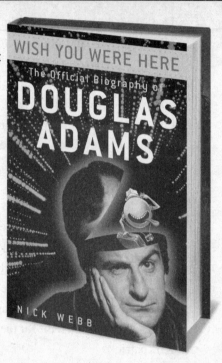

Douglas Adams made the universe a much funnier place to inhabit and forever changed the way we think about towels, extraterrestrial poetry, and especially the number 42 in *The Hitchhiker's Guide to the Galaxy* series. And then, too soon, he was gone.

Just who was this impossibly tall Englishman? Written by a longtime friend of the author, this official biography is a revealing, cosmic ride through the unique and winsome world of Douglas Adams. Includes 16 pages of exclusive photos.

Praise for *Wish You Were Here*

"Webb's tale brims with affection and humour; EVERY PAGE IS A DELIGHT."

—*The Daily Mail* (UK)